SON OF NO ONE

DARYL J. BALL

Published 2018 by Daryl J. Ball
Copyright © 2018 Daryl J. Ball

Cover by Ravenborn Cover Designs
Book Design by Lia Rees at Free Your Words
(www.freeyourwords.com)

ISBN: 978-0-9959668-3-3

For my friends, Rob and Evelyn - in my youth you showed me how to dream and put it into words. Without the two of you, this story would never have been possible.

CONTENTS

Chapter One.. *1*

Chapter Two.. *11*

Chapter Three...*26*

Chapter Four...*36*

Chapter Five.. *46*

Chapter Six.. *60*

Chapter Seven... *68*

Chapter Eight.. *77*

Chapter Nine.. *84*

Chapter Ten... *91*

Chapter Eleven..*95*

Chapter Twelve... *106*

Chapter Thirteen.. *114*

Acknowledgements..

About The Author...

CHAPTER ONE

Kar swept his damp muddy hair back from his face. After months of trekking through the swamplands, barely surviving the trolls and other creatures that resided in them, he had finally reached his destination. He hadn't been sure what to expect given he had only known the direction to head in but it was pretty obvious he had reached it. The building before him was monstrous in size, easily the biggest building he had come across in his life. Gulping, he moved to examine it more closely, hoping to find a way in. As much as he wanted to find the gem that had led to his coming here in the first place, finding out that it was almost certain to be within this building was very bad news. There was a sorcerer here.

Sorcerers were nightmares, mages who had stopped caring one iota about the rest of the world, something even more dangerous with the sharp reduction in the availability of magic in Mibekel. Their sole goal was to learn more, and they were more than willing to pursue whatever means possible to accomplish their goals, usually at the cost of numerous lives and the destruction of the surrounding area. This was why sorcerers were killed with extreme prejudice.

It shouldn't have surprised Kar to discover one in the swamplands. There, a sorcerer could go about their business in secret away from others where the only victims would be creatures he had already encountered. No one would miss them or notice if they perished, well except maybe the trolls. The swamplands were already a hell hole, and so if it looked horrible most chalked it up to being the same old, same old. The perfect hiding spot for a sorcerer.

Mages used huts located outside other civilized areas, but still, they were relatively close by. Clerics operated out of temples in undisclosed locations. Sorcerers? Since they didn't care, they lived wherever they felt best suited their needs. In this case, Kar had settled on referring to it as a lair. It screamed that it was bad news by the look of it. There was even a face built right into the stone architecture. Yeah, how could Kar not imagine it was bad news upon seeing that? If the gem he sought in these swamplands was anywhere, of course it would be in there, in the hands of a sorcerer.

There was no easy way to enter the lair, only a window fairly high up. Grabbing some vines he had found laying on the ground nearby, Kar spent a fair amount of time tying them together. Fastening one of the bolts he used for his crossbow to one end in order to provide a point, he proceeded to make several attempts at slinging it high enough to get it through the window and catch on to something inside. That plan failed. Kar simply couldn't get it to arc up high enough and across to go through the window. Taking a bit of extra time, he re-adjusted how the bolt was attached before loading it into the crossbow and firing. That gave him the height he needed but it took a few more attempts before he got it to hook on something. Testing that it would hold, he secured his weapons and began the task of very carefully scaling the tower as quickly as he could before the vines broke.

Kar had nearly reached the opening when the vine become separated from the bolt. He had to act quickly to get his sword out and drive it hard into the cracks between the stones as he fell. As Kar dangled there against the wall, clutching desperately to the hilt of his sword, he had to exert what strength he had left to heft himself up just enough to reach up and grab the edge of the window. His sword would be useless for combat now. He had already depleted most of his quiver of bolts getting to the tower. He hauled himself through the window opening and tumbled nearly exhausted to the floor.

Kar didn't know how long he lay there catching his breath, but if the sorcerer knew of his presence he showed no signs of it. Making his way through the lair, Kar was sure to check every room with an increasing sense of urgency, especially since he hadn't seen the sorcerer yet. As the number of rooms dwindled, the dreadful sense that he would find both the sorcerer and the gem in the same place increased.

Slipping into the next open door, Kar saw what could only be the gem, and no sorcerer, thankfully. The first step he had taken into the room had set off magical defences, the kind that sent him flying backwards hard out of the room and left his body shaking badly. Even if it wasn't the gem, that thing in there was certainly important if it was this well guarded by magic. Getting to his feet slowly, Kar grinned to himself as he took one of his remaining bolts and set it in his crossbow. Taking the most care with his aim he had ever taken in his life, save for when he was being tested by his instructors, he fired. The bolt shot upwards in an arc and then down so that it landed just behind the gem.

If it was the gem he'd been looking for, and the scroll's words were true, then knocking the gem loose should disrupt any magic surrounding it. Kar's feet remained planted flat on the floor. No magical defence was propelling him back this time. The sound of a soft thud was confirmation he'd succeeded. Kar moved to enter the room again. Struggling to get down on to his hands and knees, Kar crawled forward to note that the gem was indeed on the floor. Definite success.

Closing his eyes tightly, he reached out, prepared for anything. He could feel it as his fingers closed around the gem and quickly pulled it towards himself. It was a light blue, slightly bigger than his hand, and not the most elegantly cut, but he had been successful in retrieving it. The sorcerer had not yet appeared though, and with the racket he had surely kicked up, and the way he had screwed up the magical defences, he had very likely set off several alarm bells he couldn't hear. That was when a blast of mystic energy sent Kar across the floor into the nearest wall, his body screaming at him in agony. It was a calculated and precise shot – the sorcerer was here. Kar had their gem and was weapon-less save for one remaining bolt and a crossbow.

Kar had fallen hard to the floor, clutching his chest, feeling like every inch of his insides were on fire. And here he had thought the troll's vice-like grip on his skull had been bad back in the swamp. He was lucky the gem was causing the spell to not have its intended effect. The sorcerer was casting enough magic in his direction to destroy a forest, and yet Kar was still alive. It was a strange thing to get used to, the idea that keeping the gem clutched close to his chest was actually disrupting the magic's effects enough to keep him alive.

Lucky him…in retrospect.

Kar's eyes wanted to close; his body wanted to just stop working as he struggled to stay awake and fight back, to get away. He had to keep them open so he could locate exactly where the sorcerer was. It didn't take long to spot them hovering just above the floor, covered head to toe by an ornate hooded purple robe. It was hard to tell from Kar's vantage point anything else about them, especially since the sorcerer's magic had sparked up a storm of energy that he couldn't see through. The amount of magic being tossed around wasn't supposed to be available for this long. The world of Mibekel didn't have the abundance of energy it once did, not since the Barrier had been built. How long could the sorcerer keep this up? The whole lair, or at least the area that Kar was in, seemed to be illuminated by it. All he could see of the sorcerer was the edge of their robes and that became the only thing he could focus on as the wind reached a deafening roar. His body remained pinned tightly to the floor save for when the sorcerer blasted him with a fresh wave of magic. The impact caused his body to jerk and spasm violently. Thanks to the crackling around the edges of each blast, he was bleeding slowly, with every recent wound ripped open by the ongoing assault. Kar could either lay there and die or try and survive. The only way to survive though meant doing the seemingly impossible.

Stop the sorcerer.

One bolt left, his body was broken and bleeding, far from home, and at the mercy of an exuberantly ticked off sorcerer. *My life sucks immensely right now*, Kar thought. He couldn't grab his crossbow without risking the sorcerer blasting it to pieces. He was going to die; that was all there was to it. In all that chaos, he managed to get onto his stomach and start moving forward through the maelstrom of arcane energy towards the sorcerer. He didn't even realise he had bumped into the sorcerer until he caused them to fall backwards. The hood the sorcerer wore still covered their face as they fell.

At that angle, no gem was going to protect Kar; nothing was. He needed to end this. Taking his last bolt and pushing himself up painfully on to his knees, he drove it into where the sorcerer's throat should have been. After all, if they couldn't breathe, they couldn't talk or cast spells. If he could do that hard enough, maybe that would buy him some time. Then maybe he could hide in the swampland. Of course, he would be completely weaponless and half-dead, making it difficult to get past the trolls and everything else again, but he'd have time at least. Just not much of it.

The sorcerer had fallen flat, the robes empty, and the maelstrom of energy raged even more out of control than before. The lair's walls were starting to break under the strain of the unleashed mystic energy. Kar crawled, he slithered, he fell, he jumped, and finally he ran out of there as quickly as his broken body would allow. He had managed to do so just before the whole place collapsed on top of itself, magic unleashed without anything to control it.

Kar had always heard the horror stories about magic without control, and here he was witnessing it. He wondered just how much the sorcerer had harnessed and unleashed to let it build to this level before Kar had managed to hurt him. The fact that there was no body bothered him too, but it was a worry for another time. The blast of energy that had hit him as the place finally collapsed sent a wave of energy outward, throwing him halfway across the swamplands. At least that was what it had felt like to him.

He had no idea where in the swamplands he was exactly when he landed. With mud on his back, it certainly wasn't an area he had passed through already. He could tell that from the direction he had come from, though the entire area of swampland behind him was either levelled or on fire. The devastation stretched for what seemed forever.

Once Kar could breathe again, he coughed and sputtered, delighted to find he was still holding the gem against his chest. At some point during the fight, it had become hooked inside of his vest without him even noticing. Considering the force applied when he fell, Kar was just surprised the gem hadn't become embedded in his chest.

When he could move again, however slowly and painfully, he spent the better part of two days working on getting his bearings to try and get out of the swamplands. Kar's only real concern at the moment was survival.

Kar had just begun to head in the direction that he had determined would get him out of there the quickest when the trolls spotted him. He had already dealt with enough trolls to last a lifetime while travelling through the swamp to the sorcerer's lair, and he hardly wanted to deal with them again. As injured and as sore as he was, he struggled to move fast enough to get away. Checking over his shoulder constantly to keep track of how far behind him they were, he failed to notice the troll that was now in front of him. Trolls were gigantic and made of solid rock. They were monstrous protectors and nearly impossible to kill. They tended to be great engineers, but it was impossible to look one in the face unless it was sitting down, or it was about to bite your face off while crushing you to a pulp in its hand.

The crushing blow to Kar's gut sent him crashing to the ground, coughing up blood. His body felt like it had folded in half at the point of impact, his ribs cracking.

Having lost consciousness following the troll's attack, the next time Kar opened his eyes, he was at the very edge of the swamplands. He still had the gem, that was a relief. The only conclusion he could come to was that the troll that had knocked him out had decided he wasn't worth killing or anything and had then deposited him outside of its territory.

Lucky him.

CHAPTER TWO

ell now, this is a fine how do you do, isn't it? Kar thought as he hung upside down watching a fire start underneath him. He had only been out of the swamplands and heading back towards civilization for a week and already he had been jumped by highwaymen. Not exactly the best thing to have happen given he was still recovering. If he twisted his head just right, he could see the other side. That was where his kobold captors were discussing something or other to do with cabbages and carrots. It didn't seem at all to involve Kar personally, which was a relatively good sign.

Kobolds were vicious, dim-witted creatures who looked similar to goblins, but they were slightly taller than them and had a tougher exterior. They also tended to be by all accounts be horrible folks to have to work with if you needed to follow a strategy of any kind. The fact that they as a species happened to be naturally gifted at engineering was pretty much the only reason anybody ever turned to them for anything. They didn't seem to have the concentration needed to actually study it. If any of them had been able to study and use magic, all of Mibekel would likely be in big trouble.

Kar really disliked kobolds. They had fouled up his original carefully researched plans, plans that would have allowed him to pinpoint possible small flaws in the Barrier. The kobolds had played a big role in setting up the physical structure that the Barrier's magic was erected around. There had been bound to be at least one spot he could use, but finding it had required dealing with the kobolds themselves. He had even gone so far as to include learning their language during his studies so that he could read any notes they had made. Unfortunately, it hadn't worked out, as they had caught him rifling through them. They had then squirreled the notes away elsewhere after giving him a hellacious beating. Then they dumped him on the side of a road. That had ended that plan, and he had been forced to use a backup plan, one which had led to him going through the swamplands. Kobolds were also notorious kleptomaniacs. The question right now, though, was whether or not they were merely plotting dinner. Knowing what he did about them, namely that they were not savages, then he wondered what they planned to do with him. It really was a moot point, given he'd be able to get free in a few minutes if they kept ignoring him. Getting away from the campsite intact and retrieving what he had on his person when these fine folks had gotten the drop on him, well that was another story altogether.

He wasn't worried about the crossbow or other much smaller weapons he had been carrying; he could replace those if need be. As expensive and as annoying as that task was, it was still an option he could live with. The gem that he had just risked his life for? No, that was a different matter entirely. He hadn't spent almost a year trudging through swampland to obtain it only to lose it now. In hindsight, the swamps had one benefit; they all but ensured he didn't need to trouble himself with his mother's people.

That ended now, Kar thought with a sigh as someone new arrived on the scene – one of his older half-brothers, and full-blooded elf, Tekari. He was the very definition of how stories often seemed to depict elves. Graceful, artistic, brilliant warriors, fair-skinned, tall, and wise. Of course, it helped that they often wrote those stories themselves but Kar had never known an elf who better reflected that image than Tekari. Why he was here, Kar didn't really care – for all he knew these kobolds worked for him. After all, he knew what total scumbags elves could be. It was a consequence of growing up surrounded by them and not being considered one of them. That was something Tek and others made sure he was reminded of constantly, no matter how much his mother liked to try and pretend he was like them, or convince others in the village that he was. "Fancy finding you here of all places little *ashko*," Tek sang out as the rope suspending Kar was cut. Tumbling immediately to avoid landing in the fire, Kar glared at his older half-brother and then took note of what the kobolds were doing.

"I'm on a quest remember? You were there when I announced it and when I left..better question is what you're doing here..and dressed like you're going to war?" Kar shot back. Whatever Tek had done to distract the kobolds so he could rescue him had seemingly ended.

"Our mother got worried because you've been gone nearly a year. Quests don't typically take anywhere near that long, so I as your responsible, loving..."

"Cut the crap and see if you can deal with those guys, after all, you're the one with the fancy armour and a sword. My quest hit a few snags is all," Kar replied, moving to make sure that Tek was between the kobolds and himself. If his brother could keep them busy for a bit, he could retrieve his gear and the gem.

Leaving Tek to fight off the kobold highwaymen was easy. Despite sharing a mother, Kar had grown up knowing he didn't belong. That in large part had to do with the fact that he was from a village full of elves, and the only person who looked remotely like him in overall build and complexion was the enemy. Someone whose picture was posted in the village square right outside the chief's house, and was used as a target for archery practice. That had made deciding what his quest would be once he was of age pretty easy to figure out, and not just because going on one would get him out of the village, either.

He knew what the story was, why he was different. It had to do with his father. The man who had sired him, although in rather violent fashion and against his mother's wishes. The man was also the reason why Kar had trudged through the swampland and left the village. He was a human warrior who had led a raid through the village years earlier. It had been part of the war the human race had declared on the rest of Mibekel, and that warrior had elected to rape Kar's mother, leaving the child that would later be born as a rather permanent reminder of his crime. A half-elf named Karantu.

Enough bloody thinking, Kar thought as he located where the kobolds had stashed everything. Tek seemed to be doing a masterful job of keeping the highwaymen back, which was hardly surprising. It was just annoying to know that the man would have an even more irritating smirk afterward than usual.

"Watch out!" Tek's voice came, causing Kar to glance away from the stash in time to see that two of the kobolds had gotten past the warrior and were headed straight for him. Kobolds may not have been the brightest or swiftest acting bunch of folks Kar had ever been jumped by, but he still didn't want to get caught by them again. Kobolds were tough, but if they had any penchant for using magic, Kar hadn't heard of it and he had done a lot of reading about the different races in his youth. Essentially, they were thugs. Having even two of them after him meant he was about to get himself beaten up pretty badly. He had been beaten up more than once by kobolds already.

He still didn't have any of his weapons, and Tekari was busy with the others, so he couldn't count on him for help right now. That meant it was time for a little game of double-back-behind-them-and-take-them-out-one-at-a time. Okay, so it was more of a strategy than a game. Games have much shorter titles.

Fortunately, there were only two of them. Also in his favour was that they tended to be a lot more easily distracted and less savage than the goblins. Unfortunately, they were also one of the fastest races out there, as evidenced by two of them getting past his half-brother. They made elves in general look slow by comparison. Kar gracefully dodged to one side and rolled into a somersault, then popped back onto his feet where he struck one of the kobolds hard on the chin. The kobold fell backwards with a thud.

That's one down and here comes the other one. Kar promptly resumed running as fast as he could, zigging and zagging his way through their encampment. As he passed Tek he gave him a quick thumbs up.

Kar could move fast when he wanted to. But after being tied upside down for a prolonged period? Yeah, not so much. Kar ducked and swerved ahead of the kobold, panting. He was almost in the clear—until the kobolds got out its bolo. It was flung at Kar, and tangled up his feet, causing him to crash to the ground. "Kar! Quit playing around...there's no way you lasted a year out here just to get taken down that easily!" Tek called as the warrior clubbed the highwayman closest to him in the side of the head, knocking him down.

"I'm injured! It kind of slows things down, you know. Fighting and killing giant rats...or getting nearly broken in half by trolls will do that," Kar called back as he moved to try and disentangle himself. It was too late though, as the kobold who had ensnared him began kicking him with its bare feet. That wouldn't have been so bad if the other kobolds hadn't just managed to take Tek down using their superior numbers and the fact his half-brother had been actively trying to avoid killing them.

"You survived trolls...as in more than one? Not bad for an *ashko*. I already knew you had been in the swamplands from trying to track you..." Tek grumbled as the kobolds kicked both of them with their sharp toes. Kar was pretty sure they had chipped one of his teeth. They'd definitely bloodied his mouth and bruised both him and Tek.

"Oh shut up with that *ashko* crap. I can handle hearing it from your kind but I shouldn't need to hear it from my own family," Kar spat. Swinging an arm out, he just barely managed to graze one kobold's leg and send it stepping back. It wasn't a great opening, and it would only last half a second, but he was nothing if not resourceful. There was just enough of an opening to allow Kar to get a hand into his pocket to fish out a small piece of material they'd missed when they had searched him. He had little doubt that Tek could get free on his own. He had only a second before the kobolds were on him again, this time ready to truss both of them up for hanging over the fire until they decided if they were too much trouble to let live.

Kar chewed the material he had popped into his mouth furiously. The stuff tasted awful, but it was the quickest way to activate it from its inert state into what he needed, which was something spectacularly explosive. Kar hated to waste such a thing, but out-manoeuvring his captors wasn't working out so far. Just as they got the first rope secured, he spat it out onto the ground next to where Tek was moving to get to his feet and clenched his eyes shut.

"Tek, eyes closed!" he shouted as the kobolds glanced where he had spit. The ground started to smoke. This was an awful, dark, thick smoke that made Kar's eyes water. A lot. Pulling himself along the ground as quickly as he could while they choked on the smoke, Kar got his feet free and tracked down where they had put their loot, and especially the gem. He could already hear Tek taking advantage of the distraction to knock the kobolds around. Finding what the gem, Kar grabbed his gear, a handful of extra coins, Tek's gear, and anything else he could grab quickly. It was going to temporarily weigh him down more than he wished.

As Kar turned to escape he noted that Tek was holding his own, but the smoke was dissipating. He hesitated for half a minute before dropping Tek's gear as close to his half-brother as he could. Then, he ran towards the trees. The kobolds would be giving chase soon enough, it just depended on how many.

Under the cover of the trees, Kar had to keep moving since kobolds were great trackers and could climb. *Keep calm. Get the breathing under control. Do not make a sound, and above all else keep moving.* Those were the keys to avoid getting caught.

Kar closed his eyes so he could get a better sense of where they were in the woods. Having his crossbow would have been handy, if he had bolts for it. He would have to improvise using the same basic idea – pointy object forced at a kobold from a distance. Kar pushed past low hanging branches and let them spring back, smacking the first of the pursuing kobolds in the face.

"Karantu! Behind you!" Tek's voice rang out through the woods. Ducking and turning as soon as he heard the warning, Kar was able to dodge another kobold. At that angle, it was enough for him to turn the highwayman's knife back and stab them. Kneeing the kobold in the chin immediately afterward sent the kobold staggering backwards. That was quickly followed up by Tek grabbing Kar's would-be assailant from behind and shoving them face first into the nearest tree to knock them out.

"Thanks for the warning. You don't use my name very often." Kar smirked as he noticed there weren't more kobolds coming after them. "I'm assuming you already knocked out the others," he added as he moved to search the unconscious highwayman. It took far longer than it should have, but he did manage to collect a few knives.

"They'll wake up, all of them. I wasn't looking to kill any of them, after all. Now what's this about trolls and the fact that your quest is taking you way longer than it should have? Our mother will want an update," Tek responded, scowling at Kar's looting.

"Yeah, well first off there was a major shift in the plan. I headed directly for the kobold's capital city and found their records building. They took exception to which records I wanted to look at. They took even more exception when I broke in after hours to find them on my own." Kar shrugged. Sitting as comfortably as he could on the forest floor he checked his body to bind any wounds that had been re-opened.

"Ah, right. You wouldn't need them to translate them for you, you actually studied their language. You studied a lot, actually," Tek began before sighing heavily. "Don't you already have enough to deal with in society being an *ashko*? Do you really need to be adding thievery?"

"I studied a lot of languages, Tekari. It gave me something to do since any time I went outside, you and everyone else would attack me. You may not have meant anything by it personally, but you know full well most of them did. I was our village's dirty little secret, the one the chief and others broke the rules for so that I wasn't put to death just for existing. Everyone always acted like I should be grateful for that. Grateful that everyone looked down on me and made my life miserable," Kar shot back, his tone growing angrier the longer he spoke. "I'm not you, Tekari. You got trained properly. Our instructors only ever taught me the bare minimum...the rest I had to learn on my own. I'll do what it takes to survive and to finish my quest"

"Kar, I..." Tek began. "you're right. The only thing we ever really seemed to teach you was how to take a beating. You don't get to enjoy life at all, you don't hold down any kind of position anywhere, you're going to be alone forever...it's unfair to you. I do have faith in you, though. I saw what you can do. When should I tell our family that you'll be home from your quest, then?"

"Thanks for the reminder," Kar replied softly as he rose to his feet, putting his hand out for Tek to shake. "I don't know. I accomplished the first step, now I just need to see the second one through. Thing is, you already pointed out there's nothing for me to really come back to. When this quest to find my father is finished, I don't think I'll be coming home except if my family needs me."

"Oh. I understand. I don't like it, but I understand it. Your quest, it's still the same one, you weren't kidding about what it was even though it's impossible," Tek mumbled. "It's..it's a good thing you're trying to do Karantu, the man needs to pay for what he did. Just don't cause a new war in the process all right? And try to come home. We should both get going. Those kobolds are likely waking up by now," he added as he gave his half-brother's hand a firm shake before turning to leave.

Kar watched the warrior depart, waiting until he was almost out of earshot before calling after him, "You should likely let your military superiors know there was a sorcerer in the swamplands. Their lair is gone now but you should probably tell them." Turning as soon as he said it, he began heading further into the woods. Tek was right about getting on his way. He'd already dealt with more than enough today.

"Sorcerer?! Karantu! What are you..." Tek could be heard shouting in the distance. Kar kept walking, though. He'd done his part and passed on the information. Right now he had to reach the Barrier and see this quest through to completion.

Feeling something wet hit him lightly, Kar glanced up and noted that the sky had darkened. Lovely, just lovely – a rainstorm.

The canopy of leaves covering the treetops and the forest floor wasn't the greatest, but he had no intention of relying solely on its existence to stay dry, especially since he could see the glimmer of light in the distance. It meant crossing clear to the other side of the woods, but it was promising. Not a lot of things stayed lit out here when the rain hit, and Kar knew he was nowhere near any villages that might have lanterns. He had gotten rather good at figuring out roughly where he was geographically after spending all that time in the swamp.

It took longer than it should have, but he got there. A cave. Of course, it had to be a cave. The light was a torch someone had left, the fancy kind that functioned like a lantern in many respects. It lay on its side flickering away, shielded from the rain by a glass casing. Picking it up slowly, Kar ducked inside the mouth of the cave.

Entering caves was never a good idea, especially unarmed as he was. This close to the woods, bears, wolves, dragons, and other dangerous creatures might be lurking inside. Pretty much any living thing could be in a cave. It was shelter for now though, and as long as he stayed at the very front of the entrance, he should be fine until the rain passed. As the rain outside intensified, he located and settled into a reasonably comfortable, although hard, spot on the cave floor. A sudden blast of steam hit him from behind, causing him to jump forward, scowling.

Damn it! Of all the rotten luck for a traveller such as him to have. First the kobold highwaymen, now the only shelter he could find was a cave and it turned out that it belonged to a dragon. Why couldn't he have just convinced Tekari to travel with him for a bit longer?

Damn it all to the seven hells.

CHAPTER THREE

I f Kar was really lucky, it would be a small dragon, as from everything he had heard they were the easier ones to deal with. Unless they were winged. Winged small dragons were a pain based on every story he had heard. Small and grounded ones were still a pain but not as much as the small winged ones. Now a large winged dragon... Well, the heavens would hopefully have mercy on his soul if he encountered one of those.

Turning ever so slowly, Kar waved the torch he had picked up at the entrance so he could illuminate the opening of the cave. He gulped. Sure, he had known where he was roughly, and the only thing a cave could be in was a small hill. The problem was, it was supposed to be solid ground here and no cave had ever been mentioned on a map. He was beginning to think he knew why. Anyone who had found the cave might not have survived long enough to mark it down.

Lovely thought, Kar mused with a grimace. Taking a few rather nervous steps further inward, he wondered if he could get the encasement off the torch and use the thing as a weapon in a pinch. Maybe a fire would give him time to get out, torrential downpour or not. If he could help it, Kar did not wish to trifle with a dragon. Especially since they loved treasures and Kar had a very rare gem inside his vest. Besides he was relatively unarmed, tired, and not in the mood to deal with anything, especially not something that was a living weapon whole villages feared if they knew what was good for them.

There, in front of him, the dragon was plainly visible. Large, with sharp teeth, and it looked like it could crush him with a single touch. That alone should have sent Kar running. Had he not been frozen to the ground in terror, he likely would have been halfway back into the swamplands again regardless of what else got in his way. The thing he was seeing was so solid, so very sharp and pointy, and Kar was staring at a mere talon on the end of a foot. Crap and double crap. A large dragon. A very, *very* large dragon. The entire hill itself must have been hollow and just barely big enough to contain it. Lovely.

Kar took a large step back. A chill ran down his spine as his foot landed with a crunch on a stray stick. Kar grimaced to himself as he took another step backwards, hoping and praying it wasn't enough to wake the sleeping giant dragon within the hill. It was too late. The dragon must have been one hell of a light sleeper.

Turning on his heel, Kar moved to run, dropping the torch as he did so. Other talons joined the one he had already seen. They reached out and encircled him lightly before yanking him backwards into the cave and directly into the view of what had to be the largest, most menacing pupil of an eye anyone had ever seen. It blinked once. At least, Kar assumed it was a blink; it was hard to tell when you couldn't even see the other eye.

A huge puff of steam drifted up from below Kar's feet, filling the space they were in. He wanted to struggle, to scream in terror, but he also knew that it would accomplish nothing. Nobody would hear him, nobody would save him, and this dragon could crush him to death with an involuntary flinch. This was how it was going to end. Given the life he had lived so far, there were less memorable ways to go than being killed by a dragon.

"Uh...I don't suppose you understand what I'm saying, do you? Think you can put me down now? Just in here to get out of the rain," Kar said to the dragon in the vain hope it would prolong his life slightly.

The reaction was slow but telling. Another whiff of steam filled the space around them making it hard to see much of anything, but the dragon's grip loosened for a second. Long enough to give him hope. Too bad that wasn't what was happening.

The dragon swung Kar, slamming his body into the ground. He felt his crossbow, mounted on his back, break. It did little to cushion his fall. Pain lanced through Kar's body, more pain than he would have believed possible. The pain meant though that he was still alive. He was likely as good as dead, but alive nonetheless. Okay, so the dragon didn't appreciate conversation.

Kar couldn't feel his legs. The pain racing through his body centered around his spine confirmed he was in extremely rough shape and at least he could see his arms worked. Who knew how long until the dragon's foot, which was still wrapped around him, decided to just crush him fully? Kar grabbed hastily for the first thing in his vest, grateful when he grabbed a knife, and quickly drove it with every ounce of strength he could muster into the thick hide of the dragon's clawed foot. The dragon let out a piercing cry on a scale Kar didn't think possible. After that, Kar heard nothing – not even the sound of his own body trying to move when the dragon's foot pulled back from him, the knife embedded right up to the hilt. Clearly, he had managed to hit a nerve, that or big dragons were really sensitive about getting stabbed by tiny little pieces of metal.

Initially, Kar thought the piercing scream from the dragon had deafened him temporarily, but at least he was free. He couldn't really move, but he was free for the moment. At least he thought he was, right up until the dragon decided to lower its head and glare at him. Maybe it could talk; maybe it was breathing heavily or was asleep with its eyes open. Kar couldn't tell. That's when the steam came directly from its nostrils, blasting its way towards him. Being in the direct path of it was akin to being caught by a gale force wind, or as he had learned in the swamps – in rather painful fashion – like being punched in the gut by a troll. It drove him back-wards hard off the cave floor and into one of the cave's walls. He managed to get his hands out to break the fall. Kar fell forward, trying desperately to breathe. Everything ached, and likely would have ached worse had he not broken his fall, although he had definitely taken some damage. Kar made a quick note to himself to get a new pair of leather gloves if he survived this, or something even sturdier.

The dragon was moving about. Kar still couldn't feel his legs, but it didn't matter. He could still think as though he had them and hoped for the best as he pinned himself flat against the cave wall and inched his way back towards the entrance. It was slow going, trying to keep from falling again and keeping from giving himself away. He was certain the dragon could find him if it tried, as it was hard to disguise scent – especially under the present circumstances. Kar was relieved when after all of his work using the wall for support he managed to put one foot on the ground outside the cave.

The dragon's face roared into view again and damn when it was that near to him, Kar could really see its teeth. Every single one of them looked like... Oh hell, like they were sharp enough and long enough to impale somebody the same size as him. Grabbing a knife from his vest in each hand, he steeled himself for defence as he continued working his way the last few steps out of the cave.

The dragon's jaws moved to snap around him. Kar was certain he had just barely dodged them, but when he looked down, he saw that the dragon had torn a chunk of flesh from his left leg. He was bleeding heavily.

Kar fell onto his back, feeling light-headed as the dragon's head loomed over him, ready to grip him in its jaws.

Kar made a decision. He was about to die anyway, but damn if he wasn't going to go down swinging. Kar's father may have been a human scumbag, but he was also a soldier, and Kar had been raised all his life to think and to fight as well. He wasn't very good at it, but he had still been to many combat lessons, not to mention been the practice dummy for them. Scrambling backwards using his feet as best he could, he fought to keep his eyes open. Kar kept both knives out in plain view.

The dragon's jaws snapped at him again and he just barely dodged the dragon's teeth. On it's next attempt, Kar was nearly caught. With a combination of determination and grit, he kicked out hard with both feet. The act served to finish eroding what was left of the bottom of his boots. Kar was ready to collapse from the blood loss and pain. Apparently, that move had been enough to bring sensation back to his legs. The pain he felt was enough to make him feel like he was on the verge of blacking out, but he couldn't afford to. Stubborn until the very end. That was how he was going to be remembered.

He rolled away from the dragon's jaws. The dragon tried to stomp on him again with its foot. Kar flung one of the two knives he was holding, catching the dragon full on in the center of its right eye. It must have screamed because Kar caught a powerful blast of steam and then the dragon was gone.

He glanced around. The last thing he saw before he lost consciousness was that one of the dragon's teeth was laying by his feet. Had his earlier kick knocked it out of the dragon's jaw?

When Kar came to, something seemed off. It was no longer raining. He wondered just how long he'd been unconscious. Secondly, a handful of goblins hovered above him. Not like Kar could do much, given he was barely conscious and had only just woken up. How he was still alive enough to do that was a mystery as far as he was concerned. His one leg was a mess and he had lost a lot of blood. He wasn't sure why he had stopped bleeding yet, only that he had. Well, that and the leg was probably infected by now, too. He didn't know how he had wound up on the solid object beneath him, but it just might have been his salvation. He was lying on the dragon's tooth, and it was just small enough that Kar could hold it like a thick sword, and just big enough that it had some definite weight to it.

A grin crossed his lips as he wrapped his fingers around it and he moved to a somewhat crouched position, doing his best to ignore the fresh sensation of pain running through his body.

Absolute savages normally, Kar guessed he'd run into the more civilized branch. They held weapons and stood fast without jumping on Kar to tear him apart. Goblins were a short, nasty batch of creatures, all claws and teeth and a hundred percent remorseless with no survival instinct whatsoever.

Kar had no clue what they were saying, but their gesturing was definitely not friendly. He regretted not getting around to learning their language like he had others. With one set of fingers around the dragon's tooth and his other hand quickly and discreetly checking that he had the gem still in its hidden pocket, he lashed out. The pointed end of the tooth sliced through the nearest goblins with no resistance whatsoever.

That was when the fight began in earnest. They swarmed Kar, and all he could do was jab the tooth into them one at a time while using his other arm to try and keep them back long enough to do so. He lost chunks of flesh faster than he could tear through the little monsters and he didn't have much blood to spare. He needed to deal with this. Pushing up onto his feet, Kar ran. He ran as best he could, anyway, his eyes closing as if focused on a singular goal. Keep moving. It didn't matter that he was bleeding profusely. He had to keep moving.

Kar slammed into a tree. He swung out with the tooth again, barely in time. It sliced an approaching goblin right through the middle. Hopefully, the rest of their village or burrow—or whatever they used to describe their housing arrangement—were not around. That would mean it was just this batch of armed goblins that he had to contend with. Spinning around as he dropped to the ground fast, he drove the tooth straight out and through the chest of the last goblin.

The last thing Kar did before passing out again was tear at his pant leg to use as much cloth as he could from what he was wearing to wrap his wounds. The fact he still had a leg was a small miracle. He wrapped as many of the other wounds as he could in order of how bad they were. It was only delaying the inevitable, but it bought him time. Maybe. Now he could sleep and find out if he was going to ever wake up again.

Kar hugged his chest to keep the gem safe, one hand clenched around it, the other around the dragon's tooth, and fell asleep.

CHAPTER FOUR

Waking slowly, Kar glanced around and noted he was definitely not where he had fallen unconscious and his crude wrappings had been replaced. He ached like he hadn't since the aforementioned troll incident. Being able to register feeling in his legs was, however, an improvement. Patting himself down he noted a few other changes. Wherever he was right now, it seemed the people there had done more than just patch him up.

They had shaved the lower part of his face, making it all smooth again. He tended to grow facial hair a lot more easily than elves did, and now he looked close to them in appearance. They had also cut his hair and freed it of what had become a mass of tangles and mats. They had mostly left his hair long though, which was just fine. Elves tended to like their hair long, although they kept it

tied back when travelling as Tek had or for formal occa-
sions. Kar personally preferred to always have his loose
though, as it served to hide his ears, calling less attention
to the fact he wasn't actually an elf. When he was
cleaned up like this, if he stood up extra straight he could
almost pass himself off as a full-fledged elf.

As for his clothes, they seemed to be missing,
although a cursory glance around the room told him
where his vest was, and there was a neat stack of
clothing with it, all of which looked to be in far better
condition than anything he had worn in ages. All of this
told him that he was back in civilization. The question
was where. The nearest place this nice was a solid
distance from where he had been. Of course, Kar was in
the process of figuring that out when he saw her.

She looked absolutely radiant with her blond hair
and green eyes, – quite easily one of the best looking
elven women Kar had ever seen in his life. She was
smiling happily when she looked his way. She spoke
with a lovely lilted voice which stood out even among
elves.

"Ah, you're awake. Thank goodness. It wasn't easy,
but we were able to halt the bleeding and get you put
back together. Although, it was a bit of a wonder at first
if we should even bother trying because of how badly

damaged your body was," she said looking at him. Her disdain for what he was somehow still showed in her expression and tone despite what she said. "What did you do, fall off a mountain into a forest and hit every branch on the way down before being savagely attacked by a bear?"

There's no point in hiding it. If she and whoever had assisted her had gone to the trouble of patching him up, then he at least owed them a partial explanation for the shape he had been in.

"Close…uh, I'll just provide the short version…trolls hit me, a few packs of goblins, some kobold highwaymen, and then there was the dragon." Kar shifted his gaze from her slowly to look at his legs. The one he could feel didn't look quite right.

"The dragon part I believe. You were gripping a dragon's tooth. We agreed we would let you keep it given they aren't easily obtained. For obvious reasons." She smirked. "We tried to leave your vest alone, including its contents, since the first time somebody checked a pocket it burned their finger. We did have to remove the vest itself though! Something in its contents was interfering with our ability to use our magic to heal you."

Kar had to chuckle at that, but it did confirm that most of his belongings were intact. Plus, it gave him a good idea of what was about to happen next. He needed to delay it until he got some more answers. Namely about what was going on with his leg.

"Thanks, um was anything taken out of it at all? Would I be right in guessing it wasn't just me being patched up, but that there was at least one cleric called in as well to do some actual healing?" he asked, already certain he knew the answer to the second part, or at least he was reasonably sure of it. If he was right, it was definitely worrisome.

"Ah, no we were looking for some way to identify you beyond well…the obvious." Her voice suddenly lost its sweetness, but only for a moment.

Kar knew what that was about. She had just outright lied. Any place with a handful of elves in it was well aware of the identity of any living half-elves in the world, something which was unfortunately very easy to track. "But, in the end, we decided to wait until you were awake, and yes all of us are clerics here at this temple. Is there a reason you are asking?"

"Yeah, my leg is …it doesn't look right. I knew it was in bad shape, but it definitely seems off even though I can feel it," Kar explained best he could. Sighing slightly as he added for the sake of clarity since she already knew what he was, "If you need a name for your records, the name's Karantu. Pretty sure my kind all get listed as House Yanamar."

Wasn't that just great, though? It explained the nice facilities in the middle of nowhere. Temples tended not to be on maps, and could be anywhere. You pretty much went looking for them only if you knew for a fact you wanted to belong to one. Otherwise, you just found them by accident.

"Yes, of course, can't have you sullying the name of the House you were born into, now can we? You were lucky someone found you who cared whether you lived or not. A travelling paladin brought you to us. By the time you arrived, I am afraid your leg was a lost cause. We did everything we could to help you. The current one is artificial, but we employed as much healing power and magic as we possibly could to give you feeling in it so it would respond somewhat as your natural leg would have. You'll adjust in time, I am sure. You've been here for nearly a week, in case you wondered and..." She paused and sighed slightly. There was something off about how she had just said the word paladin, but Kar wasn't quite sure whether to pry or not given the circumstances.

He knew what was next, though. The signs were all there. A temple, the way she was keeping a fair distance from him even while talking, the fact that they were elves, or at least she was.

"Thank this paladin if you see him again," Kar interjected before she could continue speaking. He swung his legs around and dropped off the bed he had been laying on. He moved slowly, trying to make the new leg work as he did so, but ultimately limped his way towards the stack of clothing to begin getting dressed.

"We did. His name is Arakanar and he is rarely in this area. You were very fortunate. That said, now that you are awake, I am afraid we must ask you to leave this temple and never come back. Your kind is unwelcome here. I am sorry, but that is the way it must be. You are well aware that you are considered unnatural and the fact that you have lived to the age you have makes it even worse. I wish you well." She spoke sweetly and remained where she stood. She was likely to make sure Kar didn't linger, especially after her not so subtle reminder that half-elves tended to be quietly killed off before they reached adulthood.

It was the story of his life. Kar was considered an elf by all races except for the elves themselves who considered him a reject, something to be shunned, something that shouldn't be allowed to exist. He was tainted by human blood, an *ashko*, a living reminder, as elves saw it, of the invasions years ago before the humans were all locked behind the Barrier, a magic shield that separated them from the rest of Mibekel. The same shield that drew most of the world's constantly generated magical energy into itself to sustain its strength, reducing the amount of magic available to anyone who knew how to wield it. That these clerics had used even an iota of magic to heal someone like Kar was shocking. It also meant he was certain that, despite her claims, they hadn't quite done everything they could have. He wouldn't have been worth it in their eyes.

"Thanks for the heal." Kar pulled his vest on and checked its pockets. Good, the clerics were as good as their reputation. Everything was indeed intact, including the gem. Fishing out the coins he had picked up recently, he looked at them thoughtfully. It wasn't much, but he could part with some of them, even if they would rather kill him if their code had allowed it. He couldn't exactly afford to part with much but considering he wasn't exactly near anywhere to spend it, well, no harm done.

"Cleric Keliti," she responded, interrupting his train of thought with her sweet voice. "When thanking someone, especially when they have saved your life, it is proper to use their name if possible."

Placing about a third of what was in his hand on the bed, Kar smiled at the cleric. Lovely as she was, she still despised him and others like him: half-breeds, the tainted, half-humans, half-elves, *ashko*, whatever they chose to call them. Kar had ever only known of himself and one other so far, but it was very likely there were more. Whether they'd get a chance to live to adulthood like he had was another story.

"Of course. Thank you, Cleric Keliti. I'll be on my way in just a moment," Kar replied, moving as best he could towards the doorway.

"Do be well," Keliti responded with that lilting voice of hers. She stepped to one side before following behind Kar at a fair distance, enough to give space but also not so far back that she couldn't keep an eye on him. Yep, the joys of being a half-elf. He had to love it.

It was like that the whole way through the place until he reached the entrance. He passed a few other clerics on the way, but they all pretended not to see him even though it was likely that they had played a hand in saving him.

The new leg felt strange and it was easier for Kar to limp, but it functioned well for the most part. He would have to look at it in more detail once he was out of the temple, but before then he needed both his legs. All he really knew so far was that it was not flesh and bone. That much he had figured out from looking at it and from what the woman had said about it. He might have been wrong about the clerics putting in minimal effort. It felt real, and seemed as if it were a natural part of his body, pain receptors and all – just as he had been told. He would have to thank Arakanar if he ever ran into him, provided the paladin didn't decide he was a threat to his code of honour now that he could defend himself.

Paladins were funny that way. They believed in order and everything right up to the point that, even if they hated you and you were unconscious, they wouldn't take advantage of the situation. It was why Kar realised he could never be one, even if he was allowed the opportunity. There weren't really a lot of options for folks who didn't fit in, especially not in elven society, a fact Tek had so recently reminded him of while trying to offer sympathy.

Stepping outside, it took Kar a bit to get down the steps, mostly because he was being cautious with the new leg and didn't wish to fall. The temple was a long way up from the ground, but Kar didn't see any evid- ence of the cave he had been in nearby or the woods that had been next to it. That meant the second thing he needed to do now that he was out of the temple was get his bearings so he knew where to head next. He could do that a lot more easily once he figured out how to use his new leg out and any other surprises the cleric hadn't told him about.

CHAPTER FIVE

It had been at least a week since he had left the temple and the leg was starting to bother him less. Thank goodness for small miracles, right? He still hadn't managed to glean much about it other than it wasn't technology he recalled seeing before when growing up, but given the size of the village he was from that wasn't really saying much. Still, it behaved much like his original leg had so that was a plus. Adjusting to watching his foot placement and properly timing doing so was proving the biggest challenge, if he didn't count the times it randomly decided not to move at all, forcing him to drag his leg.

What he couldn't figure out was why the clerics at the temple had wasted the technology on a half-elf like him. Something else had to be going on. Possibly a rejected prototype of sorts? Still, that wouldn't account for using their limited magic to bind it to him. It would also mean it had already been at the temple, or else it had been a lot closer to a big city than Kar had thought. Given he had been travelling on foot for a week or so and hadn't seen evidence of a city, let alone a roadway, that seemed unlikely.

That all changed when he heard folks talking. Not too far off, either. There was an encampment, with a small fire going and a few crudely built open shelters using nearby items from the looks of it. The bearded men at the encampment sat outside their tents near a fire. They looked like folks who travelled a lot and didn't slow down for anybody.

Rough-hewn for sure, Kar thought as he moved to get a closer look.

He moved as quietly as he could but was not quite quiet enough. A hand closed around Kar's throat and pulled him upwards until his feet were well off the ground. He looked up at a strange, bearded face and struggled as the man dragged him back to the encampment. The men did not seem too thrilled about being spied on, although they did look oddly delighted that Kar had managed to get so close without being noticed and had only been caught by chance.

"Hold him steady," one of them hissed while rising to his feet and poking through Kar's pockets with one of his massive fingers. It didn't take long to empty them of anything important.

"Only a few things of any value, hardly worth the effort you just put in," another one joked. "Still, he did sneak up on us, we can put him to work. It would be easier with someone as small as he is"

Kar paled as he watched the exchange as the men nodded. He also made sure though to keep a steady eye on where the irreplaceable part of his belongings were.

"Hmm, look at him, sure seems more interested in his stuff than getting away." The one who had emptied his pockets noted. "Tell you what we're going to do, elf. You help us with a little mission we're going on, and we'll let you have your stuff back. If not, well, we keep it and we kill you. Sounds fair don't it?"

Kar watched as these men, these small hill giants, nodded and looked at him expectantly for an answer. He really didn't have much choice, did he? That and the second he refused he'd be dead given there was still that hand holding him. Sighing inwardly, he nodded as best he could. He'd have to find a way to get the gem back and get away later. Whatever it was they wanted him to assist with, he was fairly certain from their words and behaviour it wasn't anything good.

The one bit of good news – as far as he was concerned was that they had no idea of the true value of what he had been carrying, just that it was important enough to him that they could use it as leverage. Their chief interest, as it turned out, was in using his size and ability to sneak to help them commit a robbery. For the second time since being caught, he paled. The idea of being reduced to being a thief did not sit well with him at all. Sure, he had taken things from others without permission before, but he generally thought of himself as more of a rogue in that regard.

The other advantage of going along with their plan, for now, was that it would bring him to civilization. It was a day's solid travel that began at sunrise. Kar only had a half-decent sleep as he lay there uncomfortably without the gem he had worked so hard to obtain. The bearded small hill giants took turns keeping watch to stop him from potentially trying to get it back while they slept. If it had come to it Kar was fully prepared to kill them in their sleep, but it never came to that.

The place they were going was a town slightly bigger than where Kar had grown up. It wasn't elven, but an offshoot created because of the fact that all of the dwarven miners from nearby needed somewhere to live and trade with other towns. Kar was supposed to stay out of sight while the men who had captured him drew attention their way so he could do what they had come here to do.

A half-elf wouldn't be spotted as easily as the folks he was helping. This had to do with the fact he was helping small hill giants, as one might call them, to rob a ton of dwarves. Perfect. If there was one civilized group of people that elves disliked more than humans, it was dwarves. Heck, it gave Kar something in common with those elves who hated his existence so much. He might have been half-human, but they all could all agree on hating dwarves.

The way they went underground, hid from the world, exploited the terrain for riches, their short stocky hairy appearance, their gruff voices and loud footsteps, their absolute need at all times to find profit in everything... It was a far cry from elven culture where nature was protected and celebrated, lived with, not exploited. Elves looked after one another even if others were less well off, they lived above ground, and were graceful and clean shaven. Kar didn't exactly fit well with either. He could attribute that to the human half's influence as much as he disliked it. He grew facial and body hair far more easily than any elf ever could, and since he had been travelling, it tended to grow out until he bothered to shave. The clerics had recently taken care of that though, and it hadn't grown much in the week since.

These small hill giants, or pygmy giants if one really wanted to insult them, looked a lot like freakishly large dwarves with their beards grown out and the way they were dressed. They were taller than Kar by a fair margin, and he was taller than dwarves were already.

The plan was simple but did not go the way they intended. The first part went fine; the giants chatted and made themselves friendly with the dwarves. Kar got into the town by hiding amongst them making use of his slightly smaller frame. He ducked out as soon as possible. After that, found a place to lie low until everyone had gone to sleep, or to drink. Mostly, they went drinking. That seemed to be the way of dwarves' reputations: they mine underground, smell bad, and drink. So far, they hadn't exactly done anything to take away from that reputation.

So there Kar was, being a good old-fashioned elf, as light on his feet as he could be with his false leg. After managing to break into the bank and working tirelessly to pick the damn lock on one of the dwarf's vaults, he made his way across the rooftop of a tavern and promptly put too much pressure on the new leg as it seemingly seized up. The roof gave way beneath him as he fell to the floor below.

He crashed to the floor of the tavern, hoping that they wouldn't notice right away. Everyone was already loud and noisily moving around merrily. As it turned out though, they had noticed. Going through a table when he crashed to the floor, with stolen loot tumbling out of his pockets, got their attention. The sequence caused all sound in the tavern to grind to a halt very quickly with everyone's eyes turning towards Kar. *Crap,* he thought.

This was the exact scenario he and the small hill giants had wanted to avoid. The whole situation was made all the worse in Kar's view as he noted that the pygmy giants, having realised he was the one behind the commotion, now looked to be pretending rather well that they didn't know him and made no effort to come to his aid. it sure looked like the small hill giants were already plotting to use this opportunity to be free of him. They were moving as stealthily as they could to try and grab any of the riches he had dropped. There was no way he was going to allow them to do that and keep the gem for themselves.

Under normal circumstances when travelling, Kar might have been able to quickly explain the situation and avoid a great deal of physicality. Right now though, looking as elf-like as he did, that was impossible. As he was moving to get to his feet, a punch quickly sent him back down to the floor. Dwarves might be shorter than him but damn when they hit him, they hit hard. Kar knew it wasn't as hard as a troll or dragon might hit him, but it was still more than hard enough. The fact that he could even make that comparison was a reminder that he had spent far too much time being hit over the past year or so.

With so many dwarves wanting to get close enough to hit him as well, a full on tavern brawl erupted. As he was able to get to his feet finally, Kar pushed down on his false leg from a crouched position, grateful that it seemed to be functioning again. His movements activated a spring he hadn't known about and sent him sailing into the air, surprising both him and the dwarves. Landing on the other side of the dwarves that had swarmed towards him, he only had a few seconds to try and get to the door before the rest registered what had occurred.

A dwarf tackled Kar and brandished a knife. Kar managed to slip the dragon tooth behind the dwarf's back and stab him with it twice. He pushed the limp body off while he gasped for breath. Ducking outside, he shimmied up the side of the tavern to come back down through the roof.

He needed free of this place, but he also needed the gem back. Since he was still carrying some of the dwarves' loot on him, it was going to help. Once he was through the roof, he immediately socked the first dwarf he saw in the nose before somersaulting off that table into the dwarves, all while tossing their loot in the air to distract them for a second. They liked shiny things. His knowledge of dwarves came in handy for once. Not for long, but long enough that he could get to the hill giants who were already trying to slip out of the tavern amid the chaos. Kar, steady and graceful, closed on them. The small hill giants had been drinking dwarven ale, which made them less sure-footed than normal. With all the spilled alcohol on the floor, Kar had the advantage.

Grabbing one of the hill giants by his beard, Kar tugged the giant's face towards his and kneed him in the crotch with his good leg, the one what wasn't some weird technological marvel. The giant fell down in agony on top of him for the moment. Kar seized the opportunity to search the giant's pockets. He only had a few seconds because the dwarves were no longer distracted and descended on them fast.

So far, so good, he thought. *Just have to find the gem and then leave the giants to get socked by the dwarves while I find a way out from under this insane mass of smelly, hairy people, be they hill giants or dwarves.* After that, he planned to put some serious distance between this town and himself.

No gem on the first giant. Kar jammed the dragon's tooth through the giant's throat. He had to keep him down and add more chaos. He was going to have to have this tooth put on a proper hilt at some point. Swinging a tooth by itself was already getting old, and he had hardly done so since obtaining it. Pushing the giant's inert body off himself, he slid over to the next one as best he could without getting up. He quickly tied their boots together before moving up onto his feet. He just needed long enough to pull that giant down, stab him, and search him. Kar had less time now because the dwarves were coming to their aid and had clearly spotted him. Killing the giant had incensed them more than before.

Luck! He grabbed the gem from the giant's pocket and moved on from him to see about getting out of there. Tucking the tooth away, he did the only sane thing he could do if he wanted to get out of there alive. He stood up and surrendered, arms raised above his head so that they could see him. That threw them off for a good few seconds. Kar could tell from their faces that they didn't trust his tactic, especially since he had just killed two hill giants and possibly a dwarf or two, not to mention he had tried to rob them.

Two dwarves strong-armed Kar and pushed him up against the tavern counter as they frisked him for any more weapons and stolen loot. The remaining hill giants were surrounded and being looked after while he got searched. Kar held his smile until they questioned him. He was keeping a very close eye on where his belongings were being put, as well as the dragon's tooth and more importantly the gem he had risked everything to get. Twice.

"What be the meaning of all this now, elf?" the one said gruffly while eying Kar suspiciously. The rest of the dwarves alternated between watching him and the giants.

"Just a simple miscommunication," Kar said. "Your new friends over there, those hill giants, stole from me and came to your town. I merely came to get it back. Not sure about the rest of the treasure you found on me. That must have been planted on me by the giants when they robbed me. They set me up and hid the loot while they socialized with you to come back for later."

"I see, and what of this weapon of yours? This tooth?" The dwarf questioning him ran his fingers along the edge of the tooth.

"Ran into a dragon not long ago. That's a little souvenir I picked up to remember him by. Not one I care to repeat but a memory I won't soon forget. If there's nothing more, I'd like to leave town now and get on my way."

It was good to mix truth with a lie; it made the lie more believable.

"A dragon's tooth. Must have been a pretty big one. Aye, anyone who comes out of a battle like that is a warrior. Battle-tested. Not a thief, but a true warrior." The dwarf turned to look at the treasure that had been pulled from Kar's person. "And this gem?'

"That is a gem, as you call it, that I would not trade anything in all of Mibekel for. It is of personal value to me, a link to my family." Again, Kar had given them a partial truth wrapped in a lie, one that was also intended to make it clear they couldn't conduct an exchange with him for it.

"Ah, very well then," the dwarf said staring, at Kar for a moment. He pulled at his beard as if contemplating something before he grinned and smacked the half-elf's shoulder hard. "Pour the mead!"

The dwarf looked to those restraining the giants as the giants tried to deny his story.

Kar watched as the dwarves dragged the giants off somewhere, a prison or to be dumped out of town. He didn't care much at the moment, only that the dwarves had let him go and handed back the gem. Clearly, they didn't recognise it and he hoped to keep it that way until he was well away from that place. Kar placed the dragon's tooth on the counter in front of him as the dwarves all returned to their happy drinking. A toast went up in Kar's honour for facing a dragon when he had a mug of the dwarven mead shoved in front of him.

"Uh, thanks." He joined the toast before taking a sip. The dwarves were quaffing the stuff down and not listening to him at all anymore.

He could stomach the mead, but it was horrid stuff, clearly intended for folks with no real sense of taste when it came to alcohol. In other words, it was great if you intended to drink a lot of it and not care about the taste. Good for giants and dwarves and other less sophisticated races.

Kar looked down his nose at them all, despite knowing how that felt because of the way the elves treated him. Sighing, he did his best to finish the mug in front of him, a feat he barely managed, only to find another full one plunked down in front of him seconds later. The dwarves commended his ability to drink, even encouraging him to keep going. Clearly, they had their own ideas about elves, and since they were mistaking him for one, he was actually helping make an elf's tolerance of their horrid dwarven mead look good. *Thank you oh so much father, you complete and utter scumbag of a human being*, Kar thought to himself upon his realisation.

He vaguely recalled someone encouraging singing and some other dwarf mentioning that elves were supposed to have beautiful singing voices. That meant soon afterward, he was dragged out to the middle of the tavern and encouraged to sing. It was very festive, and he was quickly losing track of the taste of the mead and how many of the mugs he was drinking. There was lots of drunken singing and then the world went black.

CHAPTER SIX

Kar came to and his head was pounding worse than from any headache he had ever gotten. He was still in the tavern, although nobody else seemed to be. He still had his belongings, but he wasn't going to be moving too quickly. Every step sent a pulse of pain through his head as if someone was stabbing him with a hot, freshly forged blade from the blacksmith's. This was what he imagined it would have felt like if that troll back in the swamp had punched him in the head instead of the gut. Several horrible times.

Kar nearly toppled over as he reached the front door, but a dwarf caught him. The dwarf offered a grin. "Had a bit too much to drink, I see. This is my tavern."

Kar didn't really care as he had no intention whatsoever of drinking the stuff again, let alone that much. Ever.

"Thanks. I feel bad for the hill giants. Where did they go?" he said between shots of pain in his head. Every word felt forced and horrible on his tongue.

"Oh, those guys. We locked them up for now. Why do you care? They robbed you, didn't they?"

"Yes, but that doesn't mean I can't care. What would it take to set them free and simply run out of town?" Kar asked warily, not that he could really afford anything.

"Not up to me, but if you want to leave some coins to help with the cost, I'm sure it'll get them out sooner and not go unappreciated, young warrior."

"I'm not a warrior, and here." He plunked down half the coins he had left. Once he got the door open, he nearly face-planted on the ground outside, the sun shooting even more pain to his head.

"I'm sure that'll help a bit. You be careful out there, warrior who isn't a warrior. You sure are stubborn and proud like one. Any other man who had as much as you did last night would just stay down and rest longer."

Kar barely heard the tavern keeper's voice. He crawled on hands and knees to the edge of town so he could be free of the place. He had the gem back, he had the dragon's tooth weapon and better yet, he had his life. He had no idea how long he crawled forward before passing out. Upon waking up, Kar grabbed his head, still feeling the effects of the last remnants of his hangover. He really had to stop at some point and re-evaluate his life choices. After all, he hadn't ever really stopped to properly recover in the past year or two. His razor-sharp focus had been solely on finding a way to breach the Barrier, all so he could get revenge on the man who had raped his mother and sired him. Not that the man even knew Kar existed. Heck, he wasn't even sure how he would find the man. The only thing he knew was that he needed to get where the humans were in order to do so.

An artificial leg, a dragon's tooth for a weapon, a few items for tricky situations, a small handful of coins, and a gem that could defy magic itself – this was what he had to work with. He had heard of men with less who were considered extremely dangerous. Kar didn't feel dangerous. He felt half-dead and that he was fighting every step of the way just to stay alive.

The next week was uneventful, which allowed him time to adjust to the leg more than he already had. He used the time to focus on carving bolts.

Not that he had a crossbow anymore, but the bolts would be a start and provided him with something else to focus on. After all, a good bow could be bought for enough coins. In a pinch, he could fashion a half-decent longbow himself. The main problem was that he wasn't good with those types of bows. Sure, he could use them, but they weren't really his thing. His instructors had given up early on and taught him to use a crossbow instead. That had helped give him a weapon he could use properly, and he had learned to handle a crossbow beautifully. It had irritated his instructors to no small degree that he had proven to be incapable of making one himself. A composite bow? They were growing in popularity and would be better for him than a longbow, but they took way to much work for somebody like him to make.

If he was going to keep using the dragon's tooth as a weapon, he really had to work on a better way to hold it. It needed a hilt of some kind. He still had the scabbard on his back from when he had a sword in the swamplands, and it held the tooth nicely, but it wasn't exactly ideal long-term. He had gotten gosh darn good at compromising and working with what he had available to him.

For whatever reason, he had no idea how, but all the travelling since the primarily dwarf occupied town had taken him back within sight of the temple he had left not too long ago. It was the only other piece of civilization so far, and it was a place he wasn't supposed to set foot in. From the looks of things, the temple had bigger problems to contend with than just Kar turning up and trying to convince them to let him back in.

It was on fire. He saw a great billowing smoke from where he crouched. The entire structure was ablaze. Not a random fire, either unless the temple had gotten involved in something to change its scope dramatically. The smoke was a thick blue colour, and he could feel the heat at a great distance. All the healing magic in Mibekel wasn't going to stop a blaze like this. Nothing he had on him would help either, and even so, he was just one man. He had no idea how long it had been burning, but if it had been for any length of time it would mean everyone inside was likely long dead. He could make out the shape of the temple through the smoke, and that suggested it was a recent blaze. Could he really stand aside and let these people who wanted nothing to do with him die?

No. No, he could not.

They were good people at heart regardless of how they viewed him. They devoted their lives to helping others. Despite him being an abomination in their eyes, they had still helped him a great deal when he had been deposited in their temple half-dead. Besides, Kar was raised to never look the other way when someone needed help. It didn't matter to him if they were an elf, dwarf, or whatever. If he didn't want folks judging him, then he couldn't decide to judge them, now could he?

Running forward, he scanned the area as he drew closer, sweat pouring off of his brow. He looked about frantically for water, anything he could use to at least direct the fire elsewhere. Even for some way of getting inside, find some sign of life so that he would know at least where to start. He just needed something.

He could see the steps that he had come down originally, but he could barely see a thing beyond that. He was breathing in the blue smoke, and this close it was damn near impossible to see through it even when up close. He was sure he was going to pass out if he didn't choke death on this stuff before he got anywhere close enough to help.

It was precisely because of how thick it was and how desperately he was trying not to breathe in the smoke that he didn't see how close he was to running into somebody else. He crashed into them and had knocked them down. Metal clanged when Kar's left leg made contact with whatever armour the other person was wearing.

Their red-tinted, dark eyes stared back at Kar as the half-elf moved to get to his feet. Kar moved quickly to extend a hand to help the stranger up as well. That close up, he could see a slight smirk on the stranger's face. Kar didn't know what it meant just yet, but he could clearly make out the insignia on the armour. Not the specific god it represented but enough to know that it meant he was dealing with a warrior who had pledged to serve one.

Other than the insignia, the warrior certainly didn't look like any paladin Kar had ever seen. Given how ostracized as a half-elf he had been from elven communities, this stranger would be even more so. The paladin's skin was so dark it was almost a charcoal grey colour and his armour looked to be thin enough that it was clearly the bare minimum of armour one could wear to protect themselves. One would never have mistaken him for a paladin though. Could a dark elf even be one? "Thanks for the assist, but not for knocking me down in the first place," the paladin said, shaking Kar's hand. "Name's Arakanar. House of Maramaya...and you, my clumsy friend, look familiar."

Arakanar, thought Kar. That was the name of the paladin who had found him and taken him to the temple weeks ago. The cleric, Keliti, had said nothing of the paladin, Arakanar, being a dark elf, a whole other species of elf long since cut off from the regular elves. What temple would even dare to train him or associate with him? Those were questions Kar had that could wait for another time. Right now, the fact that the temple was ablaze with blue smoke and fire everywhere took definite priority. "I'm not clumsy, I just couldn't see. You can call me Kar, and I'm pretty sure I owe you for helping save my life awhile ago," Kar responded before turning to look back in the direction of the temple itself. "I can't even get close enough to help. This smoke is ridiculous." If Arakanar was at all like other paladins he had heard of than the dark elf was definitely wired differently from most people when it came to risking his own life.

"Ah, yes! The brave but crazy warrior who fell from the sky after fighting a dragon. Great to see the clerics were able to help you!" Arakanar beamed at Kar even as his face took on a more grave countenance. "This is no ordinary blaze, the colour of the smoke suggests it is unnatural. Someone caused this. I'm certain of it."

They could barely hear one another over the roar of the flames but tried to draw closer to the temple. Under the current conditions, Kar didn't see the point in arguing that he wasn't a warrior.

The haunting wails of dying clerics filled the air. Above it all, there was another sound, a blood-curdling shriek of joy and rage somehow rolled beautifully into one single sound. It came cascading over the roar of the flames and the screams of the dying.

CHAPTER SEVEN

Kar's eyes widened. Smoke stung his eyes. He knew that sound. He turned horrified, towards where Arakanar had his shield raised in front of his face. The paladin was insistent on moving forward, using it to shield them both so they could get through the thick blue smoke. Kar tried desperately to make himself heard without choking, but it meant only a word or two came out at a time before he had to stop to keep from inhaling too much smoke. Who knew what this stuff would do to him?

"Sorcerer...met...before," he said finally, settling on a total of three words to convey such important information. He had to warn the paladin about the level of danger they were about to be up against.

The paladin paused and gradually turned to look at him, using his back to shield them from the heat and smoke. As close as they were, they could feel just how hot the fire was as it consumed the temple. That much heat that close by would surely sting the paladin's back later. In fact, given how thin the armour looked, it was going to sting a lot.

"What do you mean you've met the person responsible for this before? It's a sorcerer? You're sure?" Arakanar asked, looking rather worriedly at him.

Kar gulped and shut his eyes tightly before answering. "In the swamplands, the very far edge of them. It's how I wound up where you found me. A sorcerer blasted me halfway across the swamps because I had trespassed," he said, wanting to tell him as much as he could without revealing anything about the gem.

Why was the sorcerer here? Why now? Has he traced me to the temple? Was it my fault all of those people are dead or dying?

"What? No wonder no one has seen a sorcerer in so long if they're hiding out in... Did you say that you were blasted halfway across the entire swamp? That would require.... Do you know how much...? Do you realise...? That's crazy! The sheer amount of..." Arakanar tried to form a coherent thought. Clearly, he was as bothered by this situation as Kar was. Except for the fact the half-elf had actually faced a sorcerer before and survived. Arakanar might have too, but he wasn't totally sure of that fact and this was not the time to ask.

Guess the sorcerer survived after its little vanishing trick before.

"Yeah, um, that was after the sorcerer nearly killed me a few times. If it is the same sorcerer, I may have stabbed him, but I can't be sure because his body disappeared as soon as I did, leaving just the robes. Then the lair came down, and a blast sent me across the swamplands. Don't think it was the sorcerer personally doing so, but I'm giving him the credit."

"You stabbed a sorcerer. And he vanished?" Arakanar began to pace. "We're dead. I'm a paladin, you're a...I don't know what you are. Some kind of badly-armed warrior or something, and we are about to head into a burning temple. A temple that's burning because a psychotic sorcerer is using up ridiculous levels of what limited mystic energy there is in the world like it's nothing at all. We are dead. I might survive for a bit, but I think you've sort of run out of luck."

How little Arakanar realised. Not that Kar wanted to count on the gem in his vest, but as near as he could deduce it had kept him alive when facing the sorcerer before and would continue to do so. He couldn't very well tell a paladin that he had stolen something and that it might be the reason for the current insanity.

"Doesn't matter much. If we keep talking there won't be a temple left. There barely is now. There's nobody in there to save by now, I'm sure." Kar tried to divert the paladin's attention back to the task at hand.

"Hmm? Oh, of course. We need to act!" Arakanar shouted, turning back around. Drawing his sword and putting his shield out again going, he led the way towards the temple itself.

The dark elf's back was already a complete mess. Going further towards the blaze, the right thing to do or not, was only going to make that worse. Maybe the paladin's equipment might help a bit. Who knew what magical blessing could have been heaped on his chain mail, shield, and weaponry – or the man himself for that matter? Heck, who knew what innate abilities he had as a dark elf? It wasn't like Kar's instructors had ever taught him much about dark elves beyond that they were horrible and to be despised.

The smoke was only getting denser as they made their way through the initial onslaught and breached the burning temple itself. No sign of the sorcerer. That was a good thing as far as Kar was concerned. Facing the sorcerer would be a problem, especially with a fire consuming the place rapidly.

Wait, why was Arakanar suddenly veering to the left? Nothing to do but trust his instincts and follow.

"Sounds. Crying. There are folks alive in here still. We need to help," Arakanar offered as explanation. With a quick look over his shoulder and then a nod, he used his raised shield to keep the smoke and flames off of them both long enough for him to speak. "Stay down, Kar. I'll try and get in. You keep watch."

Lovely. Yes, Kar had said he'd let the paladin take the lead, but he hadn't realised that had also meant taking orders from him. Arakanar nodded at him as the half-elf followed behind him, each step a risk as the temple continued to fall apart around them. The flames ate through the support beams and floor. The whole place was as good as destroyed already.

It seemed like another ten minutes before Arakanar paused and closed his eyes as if trying to focus using his other senses. Kar really wished he had bothered learning more about the dark elves so that he had some clue what they were capable of.

The paladin opened his eyes. Taking a step past him, away from the direction they had been heading, he motioned to Kar to stay still with a simple gesture of his hand. Then he raised his shield up a bit higher and charged forward.

Any one who tells you knocking down a door is easy is lying to you. Knocking down a wall in armour that was already weakened by fire? Apparently, that was much easier. All Kar saw was the paladin go forward, accompanied by the sound of crunching and crashing, followed by a scream. He was not able to see anything beyond that as the fire quickly moved to fill the gulf made by Arakanar's actions.

Kar was suddenly unable to breathe due to the smoke's increased thickness. Moving slowly while trying to keep an eye on what was around him, Kar found his way to where the paladin had disappeared. The dark elf was only just then getting back to his feet. That's when it hit him how insane it was that of all the people who could be in the area who could have come to rescue the elven clerics, they were the two men who were likely to be looked down upon the most.

There were four clerics huddled in the room. Kar was slightly more startled than he thought he should have been to realise that he recognised one of them. It was the cleric, Keliti, who he had talked with not that long ago. The one who had made it clear he was unwelcome and had provided Arakanar's name. A name he needed to find a way to shorten so he could call to him in the devastation easier. Well now, wasn't that just fortunate that somebody who knew him was present?

"Arakanar...half...elf," Keliti said slowly. Kar wasn't sure if that was her showing new respect for him or simply refusing to call him a human. Right now, their lives were on the line, so he didn't care. "Sorcerer....out of nowhere.... just began destroying the place. Fled here...save our daughter. Is anyone else alive?" Listening to her indicated to Kar that the brief period since the fire had begun had done a number on all of them. It was evident not just in how ragged they all looked, but also in how hoarse her once-beautiful lilting voice now sounded as she spoke. He sincerely hoped they weren't the only survivors.

When the clerics realised that she knew both of their would-be saviours, they relaxed. That's when Kar learned there weren't four of them as he had first thought, but five. There were two young clerics, slightly older than he was. Keliti still looked nearly as beautiful as when he had first seen her, and the other was a male. It was difficult for him to gauge age with elves, as he physically aged at a different rate than they did. The other two clerics he had initially spotted looked to be a bit older.

The fifth was a child. Well, not much of a child really, perhaps thirteen years old, possibly older, but not by much. Again, he wasn't the best with guessing ages with elves. He'd likely have a similar problem if he had to guess the age of a human for the same reason.

While Kar was taking everything in, Arakanar had glanced over at him for a brief moment in response to Keliti's question, and then back at the clerics.

"I don't know. We just arrived, and you were our first stop. Let's get you out of here." The paladin gestured to Kar to help.

Kar nodded before moving out of the way. He hadn't known the dark elf very long, but he did know that he liked to be out in front and lead. He was also a paladin. That meant, as bad as the sorcerer was, protecting lives ranked pretty high. The whole noble knight thing and all that. They were going to get these folks out of here before dealing with anything else.

They were all watching as Arakanar motioned for them to follow him through the opening he had made. All of them headed out slowly. First went the paladin, then the clerics with Keliti and her child in the middle of them. They were focused on keeping themselves healed and occasionally doing the same for Kar and the paladin to make sure they lived long enough to get them all out of there. The two of them would need it if the sorcerer showed up. Lucky for Kar, he got to bring up the rear of their little procession.

CHAPTER EIGHT

T he smoke began to slowly clear as they got further away from the destruction of the temple's interior. Arakanar was proving to be a very determined fellow in choosing the safest route possible, even if it took longer than necessary, especially since the procession had to stop at one point. It wasn't the fault of the clerics they were escorting. So much damage had been done before he and Kar had arrived that one of the clerics died mid-travel. That was a lot to take in for them both, given that clerics were the healthiest folks around usually.

The clerics insisted on doing a proper goodbye ritual, which meant they'd have to carry the body out of the temple with them. They said something about it being a habit they wanted the young one to finally learn, and how things work, and honour, or something or other like that. Arakanar was fine with it, which baffled Kar to the core. Sure, he had grown up with this idea embedded in him as well, but it still seemed dumb considering the circumstances. He understood clerics and Arakanar, whether he was a paladin dark elf or not, was right in the thick of things when it came to the belief system. Kar was the odd one out, and that was nothing unusual at all. The only thing he could be certain of was that this was going to slow them down. Waiting while Arakanar helped the two remaining unnamed clerics find a way to carry the body, Kar kept an eye out for trouble.

Sure enough, trouble was coming fast.

The blast of lightning that took out the floor around them was the first sign that the sorcerer had noticed them all. Kar yelled at everyone to move as the floor collapsed beneath them. He dove towards the clerics and Arakanar as they all fell as a group. They went down hard, at least a few floors, as the combined weight of their falling bodies took out floor after floor until they finally came to a halt in the bowels of the temple. They were well below the entrance, but still far off the ground level, Kar was sure of that. Great. The only way out meant getting back up there to the entrance and then getting out, all with a thoroughly gutted temple on fire above them and a sorcerer now actively looking to kill them. Kar had just been beginning to think that things couldn't get worse, but he was very, very wrong.

Arakanar was the first one to get to his feet. At least, Kar hoped it was Arakanar. It was pitch black and all he could see was the flash of metal. He hoped that was the paladin's sword and shield because the only other visible things were two very dark red eyes that took on a tinge of lavender as they looked around. Fortunately, the paladin's voice came soon after to reassure them all.

"We're out of the smoke. No idea how we get out of the building though. I'm guessing none of the rest of you can see in the dark. Stay close, we're getting out of here. Everyone okay?"

Great, first lesson on dark elves, Kar thought, *they see in the dark*. That was lovely. Three adult clerics, a kid, a paladin who saw in the dark, and himself.

It was so dark, Kar was surprised by the sound of his own voice. "We're going to need a way to see just to follow you though," Kar said, looking about in the shadows for something they could use for a torch. For once, more fire was exactly what was needed.

"It'll call too much attention to ourselves. That sorcerer you mentioned is obviously looking for us now. We stay close. Everyone hold hands and follow me until we have light. Then we can move easier." Arakanar's words came from the same vicinity as those red-tinted eyes.

Kar supposed there was really no arguing with that logic, and apparently, the clerics weren't about to do so either. They did as the paladin had requested and formed a line. They moved at almost a snail's pace in the darkness, interrupted every so often by falling debris from the temple above. The flames around the timber that landed near them caused a moment of illumination and danger.

How much danger? They couldn't have been prepared for that until they managed to find a ramp to get them all back to the surface. They had to slow their movement down significantly to get up the ramp without it collapsing under them.

Arakanar had just signalled that they were at the top and to concentrate on walking those last few steps back to the main level when the whole world exploded around them. It scattered everyone across the entrance. One cleric's body snapped with a deafening crunch upon hitting the floor. *two of our party are dead,* Kar reflected grimly. The sorcerer had been waiting for them rather than pursuing them.

The sorcerer's cloak was no longer there to hide their face, which revealed that they had two very distinguishing features. First, that it would be more accurate to refer to them as a sorceress. She also wasn't that old as far as elves were concerned. The fact that she was an elf didn't surprise him at all. She had some facial scars that made her look older and more worn, even though they were glowing. Kar knew about magic users well enough, but this was one of the things he didn't understand.

Arakanar got to his feet and charged at the sorceress, sword drawn, shield out, a grimace of determination across his face. He stabbed the sorceress straight through the gut, only for her to grin at the paladin and blast him backwards, sword and all. The wound he had inflicted had already started to heal before it could begin to bleed. That was troubling.

The clerics were already moving to heal Arakanar as he struggled back to his feet, going right back towards the sorceress. This wasn't going to work. He was a paladin, sure, but the sorceress was immensely powerful. Kar knew first-hand how powerful the sorceress was. Arakanar was out-matched, Kar was certain.

Arakanar went flying backwards again, his sword landing several feet away from him, his chest heaving heavily as he tried to get back up. They were all back on the main level of the temple, blue smoke and flames jumping out at them from every direction in the ruined hallway.

Pulling out one of the small items that he kept in his vest, Kar whipped it toward the nearest area of fire above the sorceress. The sorceress sent a blast of lightning at it. Arakanar used the distraction to get to his sword, but Kar motioned for him to hold back. He stared at the half-elf but nodded slowly as the sorceress' magic hit what Kar had thrown. It struck so close to the fire that it caused an explosion, dropping the ruined wall and ceiling, burying the sorceress.

They had to get the clerics and the child out of there. Arakanar motioned for them to follow him out and they all ran. Kar was left taking up the rear of the procession again.

The sorceress burst free from under the rubble. She quickly cast a devastating blast of mystic energy in their direction. Kar prayed that the gem he had on him would still take the full brunt of the attack and thus protect himself and everyone else. *How many spells did this woman prepare and commit to memory that she could act so quickly?* Kar wondered

Son Of No One

Arakanar whipped his head around at the sound of the unleashed energy arcing through the air. One of the clerics screamed, as did the child, but they kept moving as Kar fell from the force of the energy hitting him. Shaking his head as he struggled to get back to his feet, his ears were ringing. His body felt like it was on fire, but he was alive. *Good gem*, Kar thought, and drew the dragon's tooth while looking back over his shoulder for a moment towards the clerics and the paladin. There was a slight look of confusion, possibly mixed with awe and respect on Arakanar's face, likely because the half-elf was standing and alive.

"Get them out of here. I'll hold her off." Kar's voice displayed a level of confidence that even he hadn't expected. He sure hoped he wasn't wrong about this. He had to do this, though. By striking this temple, the sorceress had proven she had tracked him somehow after her disappearing act in the swamp. Yes, he had been right so far, but eventually the sorceress was going to do enough small damage that the gem couldn't protect him. It had already shown that it couldn't protect him from the actual force behind the magic, only the magic itself. Or she would just take him out temporarily to focus on getting the clerics and Arakanar before coming back for him.

Kar didn't particularly like either of those options.

CHAPTER NINE

G ive it back. You know not what you have," the sorceress shouted at Kar.

Okay, new information. Sorcerers were capable of speech. Kar had honestly begun to wonder. He thought maybe they had to give up their ability to speak in exchange for more power, or something like that, though he didn't know why he'd assumed that.

"Can't, and I know what it is. Is that what this is about? Are you killing everyone just to get this stupid gem?" Kar retorted, though his voice was off slightly, a combination of inhaled smoke and the fact that he was pretty sure he had cracked his jaw at some point during the earlier fight. His jaw sure hurt like it.

"Then burn like those who sought to protect you and gave you shelter. Like all of Mibekel shall when I rip the gem from your corpse!" She sneered at him before moving in close and hitting Kar at full force with magic arcing from the fingertips of both hands. It was not lightning type, either. This was just full on magic, and Kar had to wonder where she was pulling it all from. Yes, it was a spell she was using, one she had memorized and prepared for, but even so, she had to be pulling the magic itself from somewhere in order to utilize it. Clearly, she was not kidding, and this spell was likely how she had started the temple blaze.

"Not...likely." Kar hopped backwards and to the side before dropping to the floor. He slid forward and slashed across the bottom of her new cloak where her legs should be meeting her feet. If he could get her down for even a second, he might have a chance.

The sorceress sent another spell hurtling towards him, ensnaring him and lifting him up in the air with his legs and arms restrained by an invisible force. It was all he could do to stare down at her. She flung him across the full distance of what little remained of the temple itself, as far from where they had just been fighting as possible without leaving the grounds. Magic couldn't harm him due to the gem, but it seemed being thrown forcibly through a burning temple certainly could. Flame could still burn and hurt him, and so could the remaining portions of the temple walls that he hit. His body travelled with such force that impact didn't even slow him down.

When Kar finally did land on the floor, it was all he could do to just lay there, half broken. His body was burnt badly, his clothes were in tatters, and the dragon's tooth still gripped tightly in his hand. Somehow, the vest which held the gem was intact enough for him to keep wearing it, though just barely. A quick and pain-fuelled check told him that he would be lucky to stand and that he had cracked several ribs as well as broken at least a few other important bones. Everything screamed in agony when he tried moving, and most of his hair had been singed off. He could barely even open one eye. Kar wasn't sure if he would consider himself lucky to be alive or unlucky enough to not be dead. He still had the gem though, which meant the sorceress would be after him, but he wasn't going to be able to put up much of a fight when she appeared. The sorceress didn't even need to hurry to deal with him. Arakanar and the clerics were in deep trouble.

The hissing sound that came when he put one foot firmly on the floor in an attempt to at least stand up accompanied by the faint sound of gears grinding together noticeably threw him off at first until he remembered that he had an artificial leg. He had gotten so used to it functioning properly as of late that he had forgotten it wasn't real.

Great, Kar thought. He only had one semi-functioning leg now, if only because it was artificial. That was a start, at least. He straightened it out and used it to help drag his other leg up as well. Then he turned his head the best that he was able to so that he could look around and get his bearings.

There wasn't much left of the temple where he was. The flames had already destroyed everything, and with nothing left there to burn, the fire in that area had died down. The half-elf groaned while patting himself down to make sure there were no lingering flames. His skin had already blistered badly from when it had caught fire for a moment earlier.

First thing's first, secure the gem and get rid of whatever clothing scraps are in the way. Use the scraps to try and bandage wounds best I can, and concentrate on tuning out the ringing in my ears and the headache. Then he could see if he could find a way back to the sorceress so he could shove the dragon's tooth through her brain and kill her. After all, if she couldn't think, she couldn't perform magic. It was as simple as that.

He'd managed somehow to get up. Now, to figure out how to move. One step, two steps, red fish, blue fish.

Oh yeah, this is going swimmingly, Kar thought. He couldn't even move his right arm, which meant he had to switch the dragon's tooth to his left hand in the vain hope he would still be able to swing it. He blinked repeatedly, trying to clear his vision.

The world seemed to explode around him. He couldn't see the temple anymore. Fire was all that remained. The area he had managed to drag himself towards, on one leg and a ton of stubbornness, had been completely levelled. The temple was nearly done for.

Kar had a clear line of sight to the other side. The sorceress had ensnared the clerics and Arakanar and held them aloft. Most of them, anyway. It looked like one of the clerics was dead on the ground, which meant they had one left plus Arakanar and the girl. He wondered absently, as he squinted, if it was a coincidence that the only cleric left was the one he had previously met. There was no time to dwell on that right now, though. Kar did his best to slide forward one step at a time. What was left of his hair was matted to his head from blood. He was bleeding again, from everywhere it seemed, and everything ached. He had one chance to end this, and it was a poor one.

He couldn't swing with his left hand very well, but he could put some effort into driving it forward, which was what he aimed to do. Those stories he'd heard about a warrior leaping from above in a perfect arc, sword out and the blade facing down, as if they meant to plunge it directly into the head of a great beast they were fighting? Well, this wasn't going to be anywhere near that epic. He was just going to kill the sorceress before he passed out and be done with it.

He moved faster, crouched close to the ground. His left hand and the dragon's tooth pushed against the ground as though he were a four-legged beast. He used the artificial leg's lack of the usual limitations to routinely push off from the ground. He'd just have to drag his other leg and arm as he moved.

Gaining momentum with each step, Kar sped up until he was nearly running across the temple ruins in his crouched state. Blocking out all the pain, he leapt at the last second as he reached the sorceress. She had her back to him.

"Honour be hanged," he muttered to himself as he shut his eyes tightly, bringing his limp right arm around enough that he could get his fingers to feel like they were curling around his left hand to steady it. The tip of the dragon's tooth drove hard and deep into the back of the sorceress despite the fact she was floating above the ground. Kar let his weight and gravity do the rest as the tooth was driven even deeper until it had gone all the way through. He was hoping he'd severely damaged more than one of her vital organs in the process.

Kar knew he had been successful when she screamed out in pain and abruptly dropped the cleric, the girl, and Arakanar, letting them crumple to the ground. Hopefully, they survived the fall, but right now he had bigger problems. Namely, trying to finish the sorceress off despite his current state.

CHAPTER TEN

H ow dare you!" The sorceress snarled as Kar clung tightly to the dragon's tooth.

All he had to do was hold on for what remained of his life and hope she succumbed to her injuries first. She couldn't attack him where he was, could she? Too late he recalled what had happened the last time he had stabbed her all those months ago back in her lair. The resulting destruction had blasted him halfway across the swamplands and left it devastated.

What remained of the temple began to shake and float above the ground. Debris swirled around them like they were in the middle of a hurricane – a hurricane infused with magic energy and a severely angry sorceress. If there was one positive take away, it was that the fire was out.

Kar lost his grip in the maelstrom, his body spinning around along with Arakanar, Keliti, and her child. Everything spun around him, the wreckage battering his body. If this didn't stop soon they'd all be crushed or torn apart in the magical storm. That didn't even account for the injuries they had already sustained.

Kar could just barely make out the sorceress' voice over the melee. "You will all die! Did you really think you could stop me? I will crush you!"

She had such a way with words. She was right though. They were all as good as dead.

Kar could no longer make out anybody's individual shape because of how fast they were moving. Everything erupted in electricity and energy at the centre, radiating out from the sorceress' body in powerful arcs as she added to the magic fuelling the maelstrom. He was going to have a serious talk with the folks who kept saying magic was greatly reduced in the world due to the Barrier. If he survived this, that was.

When the maelstrom came to an abrupt stop, everyone fell.

Kar managed to crack his semi-good eye open upon landing, although it hurt to do so. The temple was nowhere in sight and it wasn't hard to figure out why. Just like with the swamplands, the entire place had been completely levelled. The bare ground he lay on stretched for what looked like forever in every direction with them at the centre. The centre, which was where the temple had once stood so proud and so far above the ground.

Oh crap, Kar thought, crawling. He was unable to think about trying to stand. Blood rushed through his veins, pounding in his ears.

Too bad the sorceress had other ideas about his progress.

"Hand it over and I'll make your death quick, perhaps even less painful. You'll die before everyone else does. A head start in finding a place to live in the after-life," she taunted, her voice hoarse, likely from the intense magic she had unleashed so far. Hopefully, she was also losing strength from excessive magic use and his stabbing her. That had to have had an effect, right?

Kar's response was to promptly cough up a great deal of blood. It wasn't the wittiest of comebacks. Heck, he couldn't even lift his head up to look in the sorceress' direction.

That's the excuse he was going to stick with for why he didn't see Arakanar approaching her from behind. Arakanar had to be ever so stealthy, given there was no cover available to him.

The sorceress spun quickly and blasted Arakanar across the terrain with enough energy to kill him before he hit the ground.

"Arakan!" Kar shouted. Whatever enchantments were laid upon his equipment, or god the paladin prayed to had done their job. There sure didn't seem to be a smoking husk in place of his body when the dark elf landed with a noticeable thud on the ground some distance away.

Before Kar could do anything, the sorceress cast another arc of energy at Keliti and her daughter. It was probably the only thing that made him move at that moment, every ounce of adrenaline he had left in him pushing his body to do so. He scampered, crouched across the terrain to intercept the blast. Even while running like that, his body was so broken and twisted that he mostly hobbled as though in slow motion. Finally, he landed hard on the ground short of the cleric and her daughter. All he could see was the fire where the two of them had been.

Furious, Kar ripped the gem from inside of his vest and charged as best he could towards the sorceress. He would use whatever adrenaline his body could still give him in order to finish this.

CHAPTER ELEVEN

K ar let anger and adrenaline fuel him. He began beating the sorceress with the gem as if it were a sharp rock. He ignored the searing pain shooting through every inch of his body as he did, or at least tried to. The sorceress might be all-powerful and able to fry a temple with magic, but up close and personal? This was a physical fight now, which made it fairer, even though she had enough built-in magical defences to protect her and cause him pain in the process. If only Kar had some way to counter the magic while still hitting her.

Oh right, the gem, he thought. If the sorceress was saying anything, he couldn't hear her, thanks to the blood filling his ears. He could barely see either. His artificial leg had seized up completely, and he was still sporting several cracked ribs. That wasn't even considering that his body would likely never heal properly with how charred and broken it was from the earlier fight, and the further damage he was causing it just by moving.

Kar managed to get his nearly dead arm behind the sorceress' head so that he could keep her pulled in close to him, preventing her escape. Kar wasn't aware of much at that point, his singular focus on killing the sorceress by any means necessary. All this destruction over a gem. A gem he had stolen, sure, but it had been from a sorceress who was clearly lacking any sense of right and wrong. If she did have such a sense, she had clearly chosen to go with the side of wrong in rather dramatic fashion.

The sorceress finally managed to rattle off a spell under her breath and send out a blast of energy. How, he had no clue. The blast sent Kar backwards, and all he could do was lay there on his back trying desperately to breathe and get up again. Everything felt broken and destroyed inside, and to make matters worse, the gem was no longer in his hand. He couldn't feel it, anyway. He couldn't see, couldn't feel anything really, he could barely think.

That hurt! the sorceress screamed at him despite his current hearing loss.

It took a second to realise how he'd heard her.

That's right. I'm in your mind. You can not stop me. You lose. Everyone loses. Die! Her tone was even harsher than it was when she spoke out loud. She spoke the last word with such emphasis that Kar was sure she was trying to kill him by telling him to do so. Her voice vanished abruptly.

Thankfully, the sheer abruptness of it was enough to bring him back to some degree of consciousness. Just enough that he could try and crack both eyes open. He still couldn't see much, but he could look around blearily. He turned his head to one side as best he could and saw the cleric, Keliti, and her child were still alive. No fire, no explanation, but neither of them seemed in a hurry to move towardx somewhere potentially safer. They were both just huddled on the ground. Keliti's back faced whatever came near, and the child pressed against her tightly. Her arm was draped over her mother's shoulder, but her fingers were still outstretched as though she was reaching for something unseen.

That's curious, Kar thought, managing to force his head up enough to look ahead.

The sorceress was bleeding quite a bit, and Arakanar was desperately trying to fight her. Her cloak was shredded in numerous places. The paladin, as dark-skinned as he had been before, now looked blacker than the coals left after a fire. He couldn't imagine they got much darker. The paladin had taken heavy fire damage, although he did seem to be holding his own against the sorceress. Arakanar's armour, thin as it was, looked to still be in somewhat decent shape other than where it was torn in a few spots. *What kind of armour is the dark elf wearing that it has survived all of this?* Kar wondered.

Pushing up using his elbows, Kar felt the familiar clicking sound of his artificial leg, reminding him of it's presence and of its capacity to take a great deal of damage. He really should look into what it was made out of if he got the chance.

He saw the gem off by itself. At least, it looked like the gem. It was hard to tell with his vision still blurry. It no longer had its familiar lustre and wasn't anywhere near as perfectly formed as before. It had been chipped and damaged but looked to be intact and covered in blood at its sharpest points. Hopefully, it was the sorceress' blood. Given how much blood covered her, the odds of that seemed good.

Kar just hoped its properties were intact. He doubted it would do what he had intended to originally use it for, not without cleaning it up and repairing it. He just needed it to handle the sorceress' magic long enough to get past her defences so Arakanar could kill her. Hopefully, the paladin could prolong the battle, allowing Kar the time needed to get closer with the gem. That was, if Kar could stay amongst the living long enough to do so. That was more if's than he liked to have in any scenario.

Kar pulled himself slowly across the ground, almost slithering like a snake. He prayed he could keep his broken and twisted body alive long enough to do this one thing. He was just barely able to curl nearly charred fingers around the gem and pull it in close again, tucking it back in what was left of his vest. The vest was more of a pouch now that hung around his neck, secured at the waist. Not that he was wearing much more than that at this point. It didn't matter, only stopping the sorceress did.

A bolt of arcane energy struck Arakanar's shield with enough force that it cracked in two. Kar did not know much about magic. He did know, however, that enchantments cast upon an object required the object to be intact to function. Broken object equalled broken enchantment. That meant that if the paladin's shield had any enchantments on it to help him, they were gone now. It didn't matter if he was a dark elf or not. It applied to magic universally.

Arakanar looked well aware of the trouble he was in. He was bleeding profusely from several new wounds. His shield arm had been sliced open along with the shield.

Magic was deadly if one knew how to use it. Or, in this case, if the one wielding it had found a way to access so much of it that they could use it at levels that weren't bound by conventional restrictions. Mages needed to know the spells they were casting. They could murmur it in a whisper, but they still needed to cast it, as well as make preparations ahead of time. It consumed a great deal of the body's personal power and could leave a mage drained regardless of their skill level. The most powerful spells could only be cast once successfully at most, and only by the most skilled mages. That was why so many had perished creating the Barrier years ago. Magic users had been using a spell beyond their ability and it had been too much for their bodies to handle, burning them out from the inside. The magic consumed them.

That was the problem with sorcerers. Nobody knew their limitations or skill levels. It was as if they had found a way to cut off that built-in limit of using their body's personal power.

Now that Kar thought about it, that meant this sorceress had to be pulling the power to sustain this much magic from somewhere else. At her lair, the whole place could have been designed to act as a conduit. The temple had enough magic to be one as well. It was destroyed, so the sorceress was either using up her own reserves, which should have drained her by now, or she was drawing magic from elsewhere. There was nothing else around though except the gem itself which cancelled out magic, so that made no sense. What was Kar missing? How far away could the sorceress be drawing power from?

Kar crawled closer, pausing constantly as he did to avoid killing himself by pushing his body too hard. He winced as he realised the potential source the sorceress was using. The temple's destruction had made it easier to see the terrain around them, especially now that the smoke was clearing. That meant a relatively clear, though blurry, line of sight to a cave he had been in not too long ago. It was still a fair distance off, but close enough that it wouldn't be too much work for the sorceress to pull power from there. More accurately, the sorceress might be pulling from the personal power of the denizen within that cave and any magic artifacts it had hoarded inside the cave with it. In other words, the largest, most naturally magically imbued creature around: the dragon.

Even if it didn't harness it itself, dragons owed their whole existence to the magic constantly channelled through them. Otherwise, they'd never get as big as they did or have the power they did. They just soaked up magic around them and were extremely old, especially one as big as the one Kar had encountered there. He and Arakanar were up against a psychotic sorceress drawing power from across the terrain, including the magic that fuelled a very large dragon's existence. That was just grand.

"Arakan," he said quietly in the direction of the paladin.

Arakanar was flat on his back, shield discarded and trying to dodge the sorceress' blasts of magic with his sword. On second thought or rather closer examination, what was left of the sword. It had been broken. The dark elf was unarmed save for his training as a paladin. That wasn't good.

"Up. Up! On your feet, Kar," the half-elf muttered to himself as he tried desperately to stand. "Get the sorceress."

Yanking the gem from the makeshift pouch around his chest, he counted heavily on his artificial leg to keep him moving. The thing seemed to have its own memory as far as knowing to keep moving, even as busted as it was. It moved even when the body it was attached to wasn't quite able to do so. If Kar wanted to run, it would make him run or drag him along with it. It didn't rest; it didn't wear out. The leg did what it was supposed to do, even if the body it was attached to wasn't capable of doing so anymore. That was, so long as Kar could keep thinking about what he had to do to keep the leg active. He used his bad leg, as shattered and as twisted as it was, to push forward. Every time he put any pressure on it, pain ripped through his nervous system, a reminder that he was essentially all but dead. It was something his mind and heart hadn't quite accepted yet, and so he pushed forward.

The sorceress could see him coming easily. She spun around so fast he swore she didn't even turn, just pivoted around at the waist a hundred and eighty degrees, all without her legs moving. She cast a fresh arc of energy in his direction.

It was an opening Arakanar took full advantage of and drove what remained of his sword into her chest right up to the hilt. The move pushed the dragon's tooth still embedded in her out through the front, where it fell to the ground. He slumped hard to the ground, motionless.

The sorceress pivoted at the waist again towards him, her eyes filled with hatred. She sent what should have been a lethal blast of magic at the paladin, but he somehow moved at the last second.

Kar couldn't let her get another shot off. He had dodged the blast she had sent his way as well.

Pushing the pain down, he twisted his body so that the arm he couldn't use was near the dragon's tooth. Kar had to force charred fingers to curl around the tooth as tightly as he could manage. He had to watch them do so just to make sure that his hand was working because he certainly couldn't feel it. Moving, essentially destroying what was left of his normal leg in the process, gem in one hand, tooth in the other, he leapt at the sorceress' back. It took pushing down on the banged-up artificial leg to set off its spring-like action as he had done back in the dwarven tavern. As soon as he was airborne and close enough, he slammed the gem hard into her open wound. She screamed out in agony. A fresh blast of energy rippled out from her body, sending Keliti, her daughter, and Arakanar flying backwards. The ground around her radiated outward in a blaze of electricity, sparks of lightning hailing down from the sky which had quickly darkened. Lightning congregated as arc after arc touched down on the open terrain, the air filling with electricity as the sorceress continued to scream. The gem was clearly having an effect, but not enough to stop her from casting it would seem.

Kar had one chance before he would be unable to hold on.

Kar could feel the flesh of his body burning away and the blood running down his face. He knew he was already as good as dead anyway, his thoughts starting to blur, and on the brink of losing consciousness. With his last thought and final bit of strength, he pushed the dragon's tooth through the back of the sorceress' head. Just as he had promised himself he would, he finally cut her off from the magic. It was the last thing he did before he fell.

CHAPTER TWELVE

K ar thought about telling the cleric, Keliti, with the lilting voice how beautiful she was, how struck he was by her even if she did think so poorly of him for being half-human. He just wanted her to know before he breathed his last breath.

"He is saying something. It sounds almost like dwarven. Why would he be speaking dwarven?"

"A few minutes ago he was mumbling in what seemed to be goblin. It makes sense for him to know other languages, I suppose. Studying them would be one of the few things he could do on his own without being picked on or injured by elves."

"Perhaps. It would be great if he would at least speak the more common tongue so we knew what he was saying. It could be important."

"I'll handle this. Wake up."

Kar had no idea how long he was out when he heard the conversation that preceded those final two words, but they were accompanied by a slight slap across his face. That was enough to bring him to full consciousness again, his eyes opening slowly, and finding Arakanar leaning over him. The dark elf didn't look much better than the last time he had seen him, but he was alive. That told him that either the sorceress was indeed dead and they'd both somehow survived, or that they had somehow gotten away after badly injuring her. They looked to be amongst what little ruins still remained of the temple. There was so little to see that it would be easily overgrown and hidden soon.

"Ah, there you are. You gave us a scare. Took quite a beating. Not sure that I ever want to watch someone's flesh slowly grow back the way yours has been." Arakanar sounded healthier than he looked. Apparently, he was capable of saying more than a few words at a time when not faced with imminent battle or death. What was that about flesh growing back, though?

"He lives. I told you he would. I know my art, paladin," said a voice that took a long while to register. He didn't place it until he managed to locate the source of it visually, perhaps in small part due to how rough and laboured it sounded. Cleric. Same one he had woken up to in the temple the last time he had needed healing badly, the same woman he had thought of when he was about to die.

Based on what Arakanar had said, it had been worse this time. It was impressive that she'd managed to heal him by herself unless a whole bunch more clerics had turned up suddenly while he was out. It was more likely that she hadn't been sleeping while putting everything into healing him and the paladin. Her child…where was the child and, more to the point, how had she and her child survived at all?

Kar felt his tongue click against the roof of his mouth as he tried to speak and failed. His words came out sounding like a kobold. He was determined to do something besides click his tongue against his jaw and teeth and not be understood by anyone.

"I know what you said. It's still something else to see it occur, Cleric Keliti," Arakanar's voice came again.

Oh good, Kar thought. He half wondered if Arakanar always insisted on putting everybody's class at the front of their name. That would be interesting with Kar because the closest the paladin could get for him was rogue, which was inaccurate. Referring to him as citizen, warrior, or anything else wasn't exactly going to be correct either.

"He needs rest. Attend to Camyani if you need something to do, paladin." Keliti's voice was even more strained than before. Camyani? That had to be the child.

"I'm not one for children, but since she shouldn't be alone for long…"

Kar's eyes settled on Arakanar for a moment as the paladin walked away before he turned to look back at the cleric.

Her lips parted in a strained smile. "Guess I shouldn't have judged you for being half-human. Arakanar won't be gone for long." She moved a trembling hand to rest over his throat, the other hand resting over his mouth lightly. "Let's try fixing your voice, shall we?" Her hair was a lot greyer then Kar recalled. He didn't know many elves who got grey hair unless they were old, and that usually meant they were well into their hundreds at least.

He did his best to nod in agreement. It sounded like an apology, so he was going to take it as one. Even if it had taken the destruction of a temple, the deaths of numerous clerics, the annihilation of the surrounding terrain, and the near death of himself and a paladin to get it, it was still an apology.

"Not much left," Keliti nearly whispered, as it became increasingly obvious she was pushing herself far harder than a cleric should ever try to. "Everyone… gone…. need you to…" She began to lose consciousness.

Kar's eyes widened as he realised something he didn't want to think about. She was at death's door.

He stared at this woman, this beautiful, brave elven cleric who, in her own way, had shown him more kindness than any other elf ever had save for his own family. Her hands remained where they were, even as he felt them tensing involuntarily, not because she was nervous but for a much worse reason.

He did his best to blink at her to indicate he was listening intently so that she'd continue and keep talking. If she was talking it would mean she was still present.

"Need…look after…my daughter…Camyani…" Her eyes slipped closed, her hands falling from him, her body shrivelling up and looking much more aged then he recalled ever seeing an elf.

He knew what it meant, but it was still a hard thing to bear witness to and he was helpless to do anything about it. He couldn't even call to Arakanar for help. Dark elf or not, he was sure to come. He was with her daughter, though.

Keliti had done that for a reason. She had known she was dying, having used whatever life she still had in her to try and heal him from the brink of death. Without any magic source to call upon for power, she had used up her own body to do so, and had used her dying breath to ask him to look after her daughter.

Why couldn't she have just healed him enough that he could recover the rest of the way on his own? That way, she might have lived.

Kar managed to barely shift his hand to move over her, resting it lightly on her forehead for the moment. Struggling to sit up, he moved enough to assume a kneeling position next to her. Placing his hand lightly over her chest, he felt no heartbeat. He even leaned in closer to her. There was no discernible sound of breathing. Her body looked as if she had grown even older in the last few moments.

Arakanar came back into sight with her daughter, who was trying desperately to drag the dark elf towards Kar and her mother. The child insisted on clinging to his hand.

Arakanar looked at him questioningly as they both drew closer, his free hand coming up to try and keep Camyani from getting too close to her mother.

Kneeling there, Kar kept his hand lightly on Keliti's chest and gestured to the child. He nodded at her and held his hand out, to let her know it was okay to join them.

Arakanar insisted on coming with her so that she didn't just run over.

Kar held out his hand. The child looked from her mother and back to Kar before she reluctantly took the half-elf's hand.

In that moment, Kar understood how the child and her mother had survived earlier. He could feel the power emanating from her, however involuntarily it was right now. A born mage. Odds were good that the sorceress had even tapped into the child's power subconsciously while drawing magic during the battle earlier. Kar felt the words come up through his throat. He wasn't sure if he was actually saying them, but it sure felt like he was. Words every elf child was taught long before they ever had to use them, the words used to commend the spirit of a deceased elf to the spirit world. That place was home to all those who had lived a good life as an elf. He knew that he would never be given such an honour, but that didn't mean he knew the words any less. He kept his eyes focused as he kept on saying the words, and felt Camyani's fingers gripping his hand tighter and tighter with every sentence uttered until Keliti's entire being dispersed, becoming one with land of Mibekel once more as her spirit moved on.

It wasn't until then that he saw Arakanar's expression of puzzlement. Right, dark elf. They likely had a completely different ritual.

Camyani looked at Kar wide-eyed, as though she had a question for him about what had just happened, but chose not to say anything. That was good. He wasn't sure he could explain it well enough. She was old enough that she would have had the same lessons about rituals he had. Right now, he wasn't sure whether or not he had even said anything in the last several minutes or just thought them. Either way, it had worked.

Kar heard what was definitely his own voice. It sounded scratchy but intact and he could feel his tongue still clicking against his jaw as though he was trying to use another language, but otherwise he was speaking the common language of Mibekel clearly again.

"Now what do we do?"

CHAPTER THIRTEEN

Those words had hung in the air for a long time afterward. What a sight the three of them must have been.

Arakanar, the dark elf with next to nothing left of his oddly thin armour. His white hair stood in stark contrast to his complexion. He had a cracked and battered shield strapped tightly to his forearm, and half of a sword sitting awkwardly at his hip, no scabbard left for it, not that one was necessary.

Camyani, the fair-haired elf child with her bright green eyes who had just borne witness to the deaths of everyone she had ever known. She had witnessed first-hand the ritual involving death for the first time when her mother had passed away while healing Kar of his injuries. The child of at least one cleric and possibly another, her blood rich with the innate power of a mage. If nurtured and given time, she would become extremely powerful one day. It was not something she would likely learn in the half-elf's company or the paladin's.

Then there was Kar. Scholar by training, but not much of one, a fighter, a survivor and a half-human by birth, and wearing tatters of clothing. The gem he had fought so hard to obtain to track down his human father was now lost forever after being used to kill the sorceress. He had only a dragon's tooth left, and it served as his weapon, currently strapped to his back. His once brown, unruly, long hair was mostly singed away.

All three of them were out in the middle of nowhere. It was only a matter of time before folks came to investigate the temple's destruction. The nearest area Kar knew of was the dragon's cave, and they were headed in the opposite direction. First thing was first, they needed shelter, clothing, money and new weapons. Heck, they needed everything. That meant the nearest town, one Kar had come from not long ago. The town that the hill giants had recruited him to help rob, and it was already visible not too far off in the distance.

Kar's adventures continue in

BOOK 2

ACKNOWLEDGEMENTS

Rob, Evelyn, Sayward, Rachel, Shawn, Jason, and Crystal – You were there in the beginning and kept stories percolating in my mind even when I didn't believe in myself enough to write them. I owe you more thanks than you can ever know.

Heather, Jessica, Stone, and Liz – You saw this story in its rawest original form and helped guide me in different ways towards what it has become. I could not have asked for better. Thank you.

To Rachel Lemons and Lia Rees, my editor and formatter respectively. You took this book and made it shine. Thank you for all of your hard work and making this experience so enjoyable.

To Anika Willmanns at Ravenborn Covers, your work as a cover designer never ceases to impress me. I will never tire of telling people about you when they ask "who does your covers". You are amazing.

ABOUT THE AUTHOR

Born in Ontario, Canada in 1977, Daryl J Ball has spent many of his years with one feline pal or another. He developed a love for reading at a young age especially in regards to Science Fiction and Fantasy.

You can subscribe to his newsletter at
http://eepurl.com/cPzqqr

You can also connect with him online at:

Facebook: https://www.facebook.com/AuthorDarylJBall
Twitter: https://twitter.com/DarylBallTM